Praise for Mariana Enriquez's
The Dangers of Smoking in Bed

"I've been grateful to Mariana Enriquez for using these stories about bugs, a miserable marriage, a provincial beauty, a
spooky vision seen from an airplane, a hot blond truck
driver, and many unexplained disappearances to illuminate
dark historic truths. One can read these stories as pure, high
literary gothic horror, Latin American surrealism in the age
of Twitter. But surely *ghost story* means something else for
a writer from a country where thousands of people vanished into thin air. And once you see the background, it's
difficult to unsee it."

—Francine Prose, *The New York Review of Books*

"Horrors are relayed in a stylish deadpan.... Enriquez's
plots deteriorate with satisfying celerity."

—*The New York Times Book Review*

"Enriquez's stories are dark and macabre, and she deploys ghosts and other supernatural elements with a directness earned by her years as a journalist covering life after Argentina's Dirty War.... Enriquez's gaze throughout the collection is unflinching, taking readers into dark and grotesque territory, yet it is her morality, a pervasive sense of right and wrong, that anchors each story and prevents the collection from veering into the lurid horror of tabloid tragedy."

—*Ploughshares*

"Enríquez again delivers intrigue and brutality in her latest story collection.... Stories of spirits and disappearances collectively address the mystery of loss through narratives that are as gripping as they are chilling."

—*Chicago Review of Books*

"[A] group of off-kilter tales enlivened by captivating unease. Every facet of her writing unsettles.... Enriquez, superbly translated by Megan McDowell, masterfully darts from disturbing to funny to repulsive without jarring the reader's momentum—or, rather, the disturbance is *built into* the momentum."

—*Tasteful Rude*

"Argentina's Samanta Schweblin, Chile's Paulina Flores, and Brazil's Carola Saavedra are a few who collapse the walls between the real and the imagined. Now, Argentine writer Mariana Enríquez joins their ranks with a ravishing new story collection, *The Dangers of Smoking in Bed*, a volume that reimagines the Gothic and gives it a wholly original spin. . . . As in her previous collection, *Things We Lost in the Fire*, Enríquez mines her inner Poe: Her characters grapple with ghosts and their own hauntings. Their spirits are low, but the stakes couldn't be higher. . . . *The Dangers of Smoking in Bed* establishes Enríquez as a premier literary voice. Enríquez's extraordinary—and extraordinarily ominous—fiction holds up a mirror to our bewildering times, when borders between the everyday and the inexplicable blur, and converge."

—*Oprah Daily*

"Enriquez's prose is full of enough wit, lyricism, and goosebump-inducing creepiness to make these stories page-turners. Like her Chilean neighbor, the late Roberto Bo-laño, Mariana Enriquez crafts fiction about the darkest recesses of the human heart that makes you feel light after reading it—uplifted by the precision and poetry of her characters' voices."

—*The A.V. Club*

"The lauded Argentine author of *What We Lost in the Fire* returns with enthralling stories conjured from literary sor-cery and the despair tucked deep within relationships. Her characters . . . dance a fine line between madness and mar-vels. For aficionados of Samanta Schweblin and Paulina Flores."

—Oprahmag.com (best books of January)

"An atmospheric assemblage of cunning and cutting Argentine gothic tales . . . insidiously absorbing, like quicksand."
—*Kirkus Reviews* (starred review)

"The alleys and slums of Buenos Aires supply the backdrop to Enriquez's harrowing and utterly original collection (after *Things We Lost in the Fire*), which illuminates the pitch-dark netherworld between urban squalor and madness. . . . Enriquez's wide-ranging imagination and ravenous appetite for morbid scenarios often reach sublime heights. Adventurous readers will be rewarded in these trips into the macabre."
—*Publishers Weekly* (starred review)

"Enriquez returns with another book of short stories, each one equally breathtaking. . . . While Enriquez's indelible images will sear themselves into readers' memories, it's her straightforward delivery and matter-of-fact tone that belie the wild, gasp-worthy action unfolding on the page."
—*Booklist*

"After you've lived in Mariana Enriquez's marvelous brain for the time it takes to read *The Dangers of Smoking in Bed,* the known world feels ratcheted a few degrees off-center. Enriquez's stories are smoky, carnal, and dazzling."
—LAUREN GROFF, author of *Fates and Furies*

"Rotting little ghosts, heartbeat fetishes, curses and witches and meat: Each of these stories is a luscious, bewitching nightmare. Each one builds up a steady, thrilling dread—until the final lines, when the true horror is revealed. I adore this book."

—KIRSTY LOGAN, author of *The Gracekeepers*

"I loved these twisted tales, these lustful whispers in the dark. There is some serious power in this writing."

—DAISY JOHNSON, author of *Sisters*

The Dangers
of Smoking in Bed

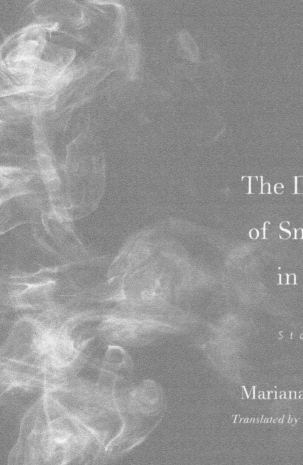

The Dangers
of Smoking
in Bed

Stories

Mariana Enriquez

Translated by Megan McDowell

HOGARTH
London / New York

2022 Hogarth Trade Paperback Edition

Translation copyright © 2021 by Penguin Random House LLC

Published in the United States by Hogarth, an imprint of Random House, a division of Penguin Random House LLC, New York.

HOGARTH is a trademark of the Random House Group Limited, and the H colophon is a trademark of Penguin Random House LLC.

Originally published in Spain as *Los peligros de fumar en la cama* by Editorial Anagrama in Barcelona, Spain. Copyright © 2017 by Mariana Enriquez. This edition originally published in hardcover in the United States by Hogarth, an imprint of Random House, a division of Penguin Random House LLC, in 2021.

Grateful acknowledgment is made to W. W. Norton & Company, Inc. for permission to reprint an excerpt from "A Sucker's Evening" from *Songs of Love and Horror: Collected Lyrics of Will Oldham* by Will Oldham. Copyright © 2018 by Will Oldham. Reprinted by permission of W. W. Norton & Company, Inc.

Library of Congress Cataloging-in-Publication Data
Names: Enriquez, Mariana, author. | McDowell, Megan, translator.
Title: The dangers of smoking in bed: stories / Mariana Enriquez; translated by Megan McDowell.
Description: First edition. | London; New York: Hogarth, [2020] | Originally published in Spain as Los peligros de fumar en la cama by Editorial Anagrama in Barcelona, Spain, 2017.
Identifiers: LCCN 2020003911 (print) | LCCN 2020003912 (ebook) | ISBN 9780593134092 (trade paperback) | ISBN 9780593134085 (ebook)
Subjects: LCSH: Enriquez, Mariana—Translations into English.
Classification: LCC PQ7798.15.N75 A2 2020 (print) | LCC PQ7798.15.N75 (ebook) | DDC 863/.64—dc23
LC record available at https://lccn.loc.gov/2020003911
LC ebook record available at https://lccn.loc.gov/2020003912

Printed in the United States of America on acid-free paper

randomhousebooks.com

ScoutAutomatedPrintCode

Book design by Debbie Glasserman

For Paul and for Chatwin, our kitten

Stay here while I get a curse
To give him a goat head
Make him watch me take his place
Night has brought him something worse

—Will Oldham, "A Sucker's Evening"

Contents

The Dangers
of Smoking in Bed

Angelita Unearthed

My grandma didn't like the rain, and before the first drops fell, when the sky grew dark, she would go out to the backyard with bottles and bury them halfway, with the whole neck underground; she believed those bottles would keep the rain away. I followed her around asking, "Grandma why don't you like the rain why don't you like it?" No reply— Grandma dodged my questions, shovel in hand, wrinkling her nose to sniff the humidity in the air. If it did eventually rain, whether it was a drizzle or a thunderstorm, she shut the doors and windows and turned up the volume on the TV to drown out the sound of wind and the raindrops on the zinc roof of the house. And if the downpour coincided with her favorite show, *Combat!*, there wasn't a soul who could get a word out of her, because she was hopelessly in love with Vic Morrow.

I just loved the rain, because it softened the dry earth and let me indulge in my obsession with digging. And boy, did I dig! I used the same shovel as Grandma, a very small one, like a child's beach toy only made of metal and wood instead of plastic. The plot at the far end of the yard held little pieces of green glass with edges so worn they no longer cut you, and smooth stones that seemed like round pebbles or small beach rocks—what were those things doing out behind my house? Someone must have buried them there. Once, I found an oval-shaped stone the size and color of a cockroach without legs or antennae. On one side it was smooth, and on the other side some notches formed the clear features of a smiling face. I showed it to my dad, thrilled because I thought I'd found myself an ancient artifact, but he told me it was just a coincidence that the marks formed a face. My dad never got excited about anything. I also found some black dice with nearly invisible white dots. I found shards of apple-green and turquoise frosted glass, and Grandma remembered they'd once been part of an old door. I also used to play with worms, cutting them up into tiny pieces. It wasn't that I enjoyed watching the mutilated bodies writhe around before going on their way. I thought that if I really cut up the worm, sliced it like an onion, ring by ring, it wouldn't be able to regenerate. I never did like creepy-crawlies.

I found the bones after a rainstorm that turned the back patch of earth into a mud puddle. I put them into a bucket I used for carrying my treasures to the spigot on the patio, where I washed them. I showed them to Dad. He said they were chicken bones, or maybe even beef bones, or else they were from some dead pet someone must have buried a long time ago. Dogs or cats. He circled back around to the chicken story because before, when he was little, my grandma used to have a coop back there.

It seemed like a plausible explanation until Grandma found out about the little bones. She started to pull out her hair and shout, "Angelita! Angelita!" But the racket didn't last long under Dad's glare: he put up with Grandma's "superstitions" (as he called them) only as long as she didn't go overboard. She knew that disapproving look of his, and she forced herself to calm down. She asked me for the bones and I gave them to her. Then she sent me off to bed. That made me a little mad, because I couldn't figure out what I'd done to deserve that punishment.

But later that same night, she called me in and told me everything. It was sibling number ten or eleven, Grandma wasn't too sure—back then they didn't pay so much attention to kids. The baby, a girl, had died a few months after she was born, suffering fever and diarrhea. Since she was an *angelita*—an innocent baby, a little angel, dead before she could sin—they'd wrapped her in a pink cloth and propped her up on a cushion atop a flower-bedecked table. They made little cardboard wings for her so she could fly more quickly up to heaven, but they didn't fill her mouth with red flower petals because her mother, my great-grandmother, couldn't stand it, she thought it looked like blood. The dancing and singing lasted all night, and they even had to kick out a drunk uncle and revive my great-grandmother, who fainted from the heat and the crying. There was an indigenous mourner who sang Trisagion hymns, and all she charged was a few empanadas.

"Grandma, did all this happen here?"

"No, it was in Salavina, in Santiago. Goodness, was it hot there!"

"But these aren't the baby's bones, if she died there."

"Yes, they are. I brought them with us when we moved. I didn't want to just leave her, because she cried every night, poor thing. And if she cried when we were close by, just imagine how she'd cry if she was all alone, abandoned! So I brought her. She was nothing but little bones by then, and I put her in a bag and buried her out back. Not even your grandpa knew. Or your great-grandma, no one. It's just that I was the only one who heard her cry. Well, your great-grandpa heard too, but he played dumb."

"And does the baby cry here?"

"Only when it rains."

Later I asked my dad if the story of the little angel baby was true, and he said my grandma was very old and could talk some nonsense. He didn't seem all that convinced, though, or maybe the conversation made him uncomfortable. Then Grandma died, the house was sold, I went to live alone with no husband or children, my dad moved to an apartment in Balvanera, and I forgot all about the angel baby.

Until she appeared in my apartment ten years later, crying beside my bed one stormy night.

The angel baby doesn't look like a ghost. She doesn't float and she isn't pale and she doesn't wear a white dress. She's half rotted away, and she doesn't talk. The first time she appeared, I thought it was a nightmare and I tried to wake up.

When I couldn't do it and I started to realize she was real, I screamed and cried and pulled the sheets over my head, my eyes squeezed tight and my hands over my ears so I couldn't hear her—at that point I didn't know she was mute. But when I came out from under there some hours later, the angel baby was still there, the remnants of an old blanket draped over her shoulders like a poncho. She was pointing her finger toward the outside, toward the window and the street, and that's how I realized it was daytime. It's weird to see a dead person during the day. I asked her what she wanted, but all she did was keep on pointing, like we were in a horror movie.

I got up and ran to the kitchen to get the gloves I used for washing dishes. The angel baby followed me. And that was only the first sign of her demanding personality. I didn't hesitate. I put the gloves on and grabbed her little neck and squeezed. It's not exactly practical to try and strangle a dead person, but a girl can't be desperate and reasonable at the same time. I didn't even make her cough; I just got some bits of decomposing flesh stuck to my gloved fingers, and her trachea was left in full view.

So far, I had no idea that this was Angelita, my grandmother's sister. I kept squeezing my eyes shut to see if she would disappear or I would wake up. When that didn't work, I walked around behind her and I saw, hanging from the yellowed remains of what I now know was her pink shroud, two rudimentary little cardboard wings that had chicken feathers glued to them. Those should have disintegrated after all these years, I thought, and then I laughed a little hysterically and told myself that I had a dead baby in my kitchen, that it was my great-aunt and she could walk, even though judging by her size she hadn't lived more than three months. I had to definitively stop thinking in terms of what was possible and what wasn't.

I asked if she was my great-aunt Angelita—since there hadn't been time to register her with a legal name (those were different times), they always called her by that generic name. That's how I learned that even though she didn't speak, she could reply by nodding. So my grandmother had been telling the truth, I thought: the bones I'd dug up when I was a kid weren't from any chicken coop, they were the little bones of Grandma's sister.

It was a mystery what Angelita wanted, because she didn't do anything but nod or shake her head. But she sure did want something, and badly, because not only did she constantly keep pointing, she wouldn't leave me alone. She followed me all over the house: she waited for me behind the curtain when I showered, she sat on the bidet anytime I was on the toilet, she stood beside the fridge while I washed dishes, and she sat beside my chair when I worked at the computer.

I went about my life more or less normally for the first week. I thought maybe the whole thing was a hallucination brought on by stress, and that she would eventually disappear. I asked for some days off work; I took sleeping pills. But the angel baby was still there, waiting beside the bed for me to wake up. Some friends came to visit me. At first I didn't want to answer their messages or let them in, but eventually I agreed to see them, to keep them from worrying even more. I claimed mental exhaustion, and they understood; "You've been working like a slave," they told me. None of them saw the angel baby. The first time my friend Marina came to visit me, I stuck the angel in the closet. But to my horror and disgust, she escaped and sat right down on the arm of the sofa with that ugly, rotting, gray-green face of hers. Marina never knew.

Not long after that, I took the angel baby out into the street. Nothing. Except for that one man who glanced at her in passing and then turned around and looked again and his face crumpled—his blood pressure must have dropped; or the lady who started running straight away and almost got hit by the 45 bus in Calle Chacabuco. Some people must see her, I figured, but it sure wasn't many. To save them from the shock, when we went out together—or rather, when she followed me out and I had no choice but to let her—I used a kind of backpack to carry her (it's gross to see her walk—she's so little, it's unnatural). I also bought her a bandage to use as a mask, the kind burn victims use to cover their scars. Now when people see her, they're disgusted, but they also feel compassion and pity. They see a very sick or injured baby, but not a dead baby.

If only Dad could see me now, I thought. He had always complained that he was going to die without grandchildren (and he did die without grandchildren, I disappointed him in that and in many other ways). I bought her toys to play with, dolls and plastic dice and pacifiers she could chew on, but she didn't seem to like anything very much, she just kept on with that damned finger pointing south—that's what I realized, it was always southward—morning, noon, and night. I talked to her and asked her questions, but she just wasn't a very good communicator.

Until one morning she turned up with a photo of my childhood home, the house where I had found her little bones in the backyard. She got it from the box where I keep old photos: disgusting, she left all the other pictures stained with her rotten flesh that peeled off, damp and slimy. Now she was pointing at the picture of the house, really insistent. "You want to go there?" I asked her, and she nodded yes. I explained that the house no longer belonged to us, that we'd sold it, and she nodded again.

I loaded her into the backpack with her mask on and we took the 15 bus to Avellaneda. When we're traveling, she doesn't look out the window or around at other people, she doesn't do anything to entertain herself; the outside world matters as much to her as the toys I bought her. I carried her sitting on my lap so she'd be comfortable, though I don't know if it's possible for her to be uncomfortable, or if that concept even means anything to her; I don't know what she feels. All I know is that she isn't evil, and that I was afraid of her at first, but I'm not anymore.

We reached the house that used to be mine at around four in the afternoon. As always in summer, a heavy smell of the Riachuelo River and gasoline hung over Avenida Mitre, mixed with the stench of garbage. We walked across the plaza and past the Itoiz hospital, where my grandmother had died, and finally we went around the Racing stadium. Two blocks past the field we came to my old house. But what to do now that I was at the door? Ask the new owners to let me in? With what excuse? I hadn't even thought about that. Clearly, carrying a dead baby around everywhere I went had affected my mind.

It was Angelita who took charge of the situation, pointing her finger. We didn't need to go inside. We could peer into the backyard over the dividing wall; that was all she wanted—to see the backyard. The two of us looked in as I held her up—the wall was pretty low, it must have been poorly made. There, where the earthen square of our backyard used to be, was a blue plastic swimming pool set into the ground. Apparently, they'd dug up all the earth to make the hole, and who knows where they'd thrown the angel baby's bones, shaken up, lost. I felt bad for her, poor little thing, and I told her I was really sorry, but I couldn't fix this for her. I even told her I regretted not having dug up her bones again when the house was sold, so I could rebury them in some quiet place, or close to the family if that's what she wanted. I mean, how hard would it have been to put them in a box or a flowerpot, and bring them home with me! I'd treated her badly and I apologized. Angelita nodded yes. I understood that she forgave me. I asked her if now she was at peace and if she would leave, if she was going to leave me alone. She shook her head no. Okay, I replied, and since her answer didn't sit well with me, I started walking fast toward the 15 bus stop. I made her run after me on her bare little feet that, rotten as they were, left her little white bones in view.

Our Lady of the Quarry

Silvia lived alone in a rented apartment of her own, with a five-foot-tall pot plant on the balcony and a giant bedroom with a mattress on the floor. She had her own office at the Ministry of Education and a salary; she dyed her long hair jet black and wore Hindu shirts with sleeves wide at the wrists and silver thread that shimmered in the sun. She had the provincial last name of Olavarría and a cousin who had disappeared mysteriously while traveling around Mexico. She was our "grown-up" friend, the one who took care of us when we went out and who let us use her place to smoke weed and meet up with boys. But we wanted her ruined, helpless, destroyed. Because Silvia always knew more: If one of us discovered Frida Kahlo, oh, Silvia had already visited

Frida's house with her cousin in Mexico, before he disappeared. If we tried a new drug, she had already overdosed on the same substance. If we discovered a band we liked, she had already *gotten over* being a fan of the same group. We hated that she had long, heavy, straight hair, colored with a dye we couldn't find in any normal beauty salon. What brand was it? She probably would have told us, but we would never ask. We hated that she always had money, enough for another beer, another twenty-five grams, another pizza. How was it possible? She said that in addition to her salary she had access to her father's account; he was rich, she never saw him, and he hadn't recognized paternity, but he did deposit money for her in the bank. It was a lie, surely. As much a lie as when she said her sister was a model: we'd seen the girl when she came to visit Silvia and she wasn't worth three shits, a runty little skank with a big ass and wild curls plastered with gel that couldn't have gotten any more greasy. I'm talking low-class—that girl couldn't dream of walking a runway.

But above all we wanted her brought down because Diego liked her. We'd met Diego in Bariloche on our senior class trip. He was thin and had bushy eyebrows, and he always wore a different Rolling Stones shirt (one with the tongue, another with the cover of *Tattoo You*, another with Jagger clutching a microphone whose cord morphed into a snake). Diego played us songs on the acoustic guitar after the horseback ride when it got dark near Cerro Catedral, and later on in the hotel he showed us the precise measurements of vodka and orange juice to make a good screwdriver. He was nice to us, but he only wanted to kiss us, he wouldn't sleep with us, maybe because he was older (he'd repeated a grade, he was eighteen), or maybe he just didn't like us that way. Then, once we were back in Buenos Aires, we called to invite him to a party. He paid attention to us for a while, until Silvia started chatting him up. And from then on he kept treating us well, it's true, but Silvia totally took over and kept him enthralled (or overwhelmed: opinions were divided), telling stories about Mexico and peyote and sugar skulls. She was older too, she'd been out of high school for two years. Diego hadn't traveled much, but he wanted to go backpacking in the north that year. Silvia had already made that trip (of course!), and she gave him advice, telling him to call her for recommendations on cheap hotels and families who would rent out rooms, and he bought every word, in spite of the fact that Silvia didn't have a single photo, not one, as proof of that trip or any other (she was quite the traveler).

Silvia was the one who came up with the idea of the quarry pools that summer, and we had to give it to her, it was a really good idea. Silvia hated public pools and country club pools, even the pools at estates or weekend houses: she said the water wasn't fresh, she always felt like it was stagnant. Since the nearest river was polluted, she didn't have anywhere to swim. We were all like, "Who does Silvia think she is, she acts like she was born on a beach in the south of France." But Diego listened to her explanation of why she wanted "fresh" water and he was totally in agreement. They talked a little more about oceans and waterfalls and streams, and then Silvia mentioned the quarry pools. Someone at her work had told her you could find a ton of them off the southern highway, and that people hardly ever went swimming there because they were scared, supposedly the pools were dangerous. And that's where she suggested we all go the next weekend, and we agreed right away because we knew Diego would say yes, and we didn't want the two of them going alone. Maybe if he saw how ugly her body was—she had some really tubby legs, which she claimed were because she'd played hockey when she was little, but half of us had played hockey too, and none of us had those big ham hocks. Plus she had a flat ass and broad hips, which was why jeans never fit her well. If he saw those defects (plus the black hairs she never really got rid of—maybe she couldn't pull them out down to the root, she was really dark), maybe Diego would stop liking Silvia and finally pay attention to us.

She asked around a little and decided we had to go to the Virgin's Pool, which was the best, the cleanest. It was also the biggest, deepest, and most dangerous of all. It was really far, almost at the end of the 307 route, after the bus merged onto the highway. The Virgin's Pool was special, people said, because almost no one ever went there. The danger that kept swimmers away wasn't how deep it was: it was the owner. Apparently someone had bought the place, and we accepted that: none of us knew what a quarry pool was good for or if it could be bought, but still, it didn't strike us as odd that the pool would have an owner, and we understood why this owner wouldn't want strangers swimming on his property.

It was said that when there were trespassers, the owner would drive out from behind a hill and start shooting. Sometimes he also set his dogs on them. He had decorated his private quarry pool with a giant altar, a grotto for the Virgin on one side of the main pool. You could reach it by going around the pool along a dirt path to the right, a path that started at an improvised entrance from the road, marked by a narrow iron arch. On the other side was the hill over which the owner's truck could appear at any moment. The water in front of the Virgin was still and black. On the near side, there was a little beach of clayey dirt.

We went every Saturday that January. The heat was torrid and the water was so cold: it was like sinking into a miracle. We even forgot Diego and Silvia a little. They had also forgotten each other, enchanted by the coolness and secrecy. We tried to keep quiet, to not make any racket that could wake the hidden owner. We never saw anyone else, although sometimes other people were at the bus stop on the way back, and they must have assumed we were coming from the quarry because of our wet hair and the smell that stuck to our skin, a scent of rock and salt. Once, the bus driver said something strange to us: that we should watch out for wild dogs on the loose. We shivered, but the next weekend we were as alone as ever, we didn't even hear a distant bark.

And we could see that Diego was starting to take an interest in our golden thighs, our slender ankles, our flat stomachs. He still kept closer to Silvia and he still seemed fascinated, even if by then he'd realized that we were much, much prettier. The problem was that the two of them were very good swimmers, and although they played with us in the water and taught us a few things, sometimes they got bored and swam off with fast, precise strokes. It was impossible to catch up with them. The pool was really huge; we'd stay close to the shore and watch their two heads bobbing on the surface, and we could see their lips moving but had no idea what they were saying. They laughed a lot, that's for sure, and Silvia's laugh was raucous and we had to tell her to keep it down. The two of them looked so happy. We knew that very soon they would remember how much they liked each other, and that the summer coolness near the highway was temporary. We had to put a stop to it. *We* had found Diego, and she couldn't keep everything for herself.

Diego looked better every day. The first time he took off his shirt, we discovered that his shoulders were strong and hunched, and his back was narrow and had a sandy color, just above his pants, that was simply beautiful. He taught us to make a roach clip out of a matchbook, and he watched out for us to make sure we didn't get in the water when we were too crazy—he didn't want us getting high and drowning. He ripped CDs of the bands that according to him we just had to hear, and later he'd quiz us; it was adorable how he got all happy when he could tell we'd really liked one of his favorites. We listened devotedly and looked for messages—was he trying to tell us something? Just in case, we even used a dictionary to translate the songs that were in English; we'd read them to each other over the phone and discuss them. It was very confusing—there were all kinds of conflicting messages.

All speculation was brought to an abrupt halt—as if a cold knife had sliced through our spines—when we found out that Silvia and Diego were dating. When! How! They were older, they didn't have curfews, Silvia had her own apartment, how stupid we were to apply our little-kid limitations to them. We snuck out a lot, sure, but we were controlled by schedules, cellphones, and parents who all knew each other and drove us places—out dancing or to the rec center, friends' houses, home.

The details came soon enough, and they were nothing spectacular. Silvia and Diego had been seeing each other without us for a while; at night, in effect, but sometimes he went to pick her up at the Ministry and they went for a drink, and other times they slept together at her apartment. No doubt they smoked pot from Silvia's plant in bed after sex. We were sixteen, and some of us hadn't had sex yet, it was terrible. We'd sucked cock, yes, we were quite good at that, but fucking, only some of us had done that. Oh, we just hated it. We wanted Diego for ourselves. Not as our boyfriend, we just wanted him to screw us, to teach us sex the same way he taught us about rock and roll, making drinks, and the butterfly stroke.

Of all of us, Natalia was the most obsessed. She was still a virgin. She said she was saving herself for someone who was worth it, and Diego was worth it. And once she got something into her head, she'd hardly ever back down. Once, she'd taken twenty of her mom's pills when her parents had forbidden her from going dancing for a week—her grades were a disaster. In the end they let her go dancing, but they also sent her to a psychologist. Natalia skipped the sessions and spent the money on stuff for herself. With Diego, she wanted something special. She didn't want to throw herself at him. She wanted him to want her, to like her, she wanted to drive him crazy. But at parties, when she went to talk to him, Diego flashed her a smile and went on with his conversation with whichever of us he was talking to. He didn't answer her calls, and if he did, the conversations were always languid and he was always the one to end them. At the quarry pool he didn't stare at her body, her long, strong legs and firm ass, or else he looked at her like he would a pretty boring plant—a ficus, for example. Now, *that* Natalia couldn't believe. She didn't know how to swim, but she got wet near the shore and then came out of the water with her yellow swimsuit stuck to her tan body so tight you could see her nipples, hard from the cold water. And Natalia knew that any other boy who saw her would kill himself jacking off, but not Diego, no—he preferred that flat-assed skank! We all agreed it was incomprehensible.

One afternoon, when we were on our way to PE class, Natalia told us she'd put menstrual blood in Diego's coffee. She'd done it at Silvia's house—where else! It was just the three of them, and at one point Diego and Silvia went to the kitchen for a few minutes to get coffee and cookies; the coffee was already served on the table. Real quick, Natalia poured in the blood she'd managed to collect—very little—in a tiny bottle from a perfume sample. She'd wrung out the blood from cotton gauze, which was disgusting; she normally used pads or tampons, the cotton was just so she could get the blood. She diluted it a little in water, but she said it should work all the same. She'd gotten the technique from a parapsychology book, which claimed that while the method was not very hygienic, it was an infallible way to snag your beloved.

It didn't work. A week after Diego drank Natalia's blood, Silvia herself told us they were dating, it was official. The next time we saw them, they couldn't keep their hands off each other. That weekend when we went to the quarry pool they were holding hands, and we just couldn't understand it. We couldn't understand it. The red bikini with hearts on one of us; the super-flat stomach with a belly button piercing on another; the exquisite haircut that fell just so over the face, legs without a single hair, underarms like marble. And he preferred her? Why? Because he screwed her? But we wanted to screw too, that was *all* we wanted! How could he not realize, when we sat on his lap and pressed our asses into him, or tried to brush our hands against his dick like on accident? Or when we laughed near his mouth, showing our tongues. Why didn't we just throw ourselves at him, once and for all? Because it was true for all of us, it wasn't just an obsession of Natalia's: we wanted Diego to choose us. We wanted to be with him still wet from the cold quarry water, to fuck him one after the other as he lay on the little beach, to wait for the owner's gunshots and run to the highway half-naked under a rain of bullets.

But no. There we were in all our glory, and he was over kissing on old, flat-ass Silvia. The sun was burning and flat-ass Silvia's nose was peeling, she used the crappiest sunscreen, she was a disaster. We, though, were impeccable. At one point, Diego seemed to realize. He looked at us differently, as if comprehending he was with an ugly skank. And he said, "Why don't we swim over to the Virgin?" Natalia went pale, because she didn't know how to swim. The rest of us did, but we didn't dare cross the quarry, so long and deep and if we started to drown there was no one to save us, we were in the middle of nowhere. Diego read our thoughts: "How about Sil and I swim over, you guys walk along the edge and we'll meet there. I want to see the altar up close. Are you up for it?"

We said yes, sure, though we were concerned because if he was calling her "Sil" then maybe our impression that he was looking at us differently was wrong, and we were just so desperate for it to be true that we were going kind of crazy. We started to walk. Getting around the quarry wasn't easy: it seemed much smaller when you were sitting on the little beach. It was huge. It must have been three blocks long. Diego and Silvia went faster than us, and we saw their dark heads appear at intervals, shining golden under the sun, so luminous, and their arms plowing slippery through the water. At one point they had to stop, and we watched from the shore—under the sun, dust plastered to our bodies with sweat, some of us with headaches from the heat and the harsh light in our eyes, walking as if uphill—we saw them stop and talk, and Silvia laughed, throwing her head back and treading water with her arms to stay afloat. It was too far to swim in one go, they weren't professionals. But Natalia got the feeling that they didn't stop just because they were tired, she thought they were plotting something. "That bitch has something up her sleeve," she said, and she kept walking toward the Virgin we could barely see inside the grotto.

Diego and Silvia reached the Virgin's grotto just as we were turning right to walk the final fifty yards. They must have seen the way we were panting, our armpits stinking like onion and our hair stuck to our temples. They looked at us closely, laughed the same way they had when they'd stopped swimming, and then they jumped right back into the water and started swimming as fast as they could back to the little beach. Just like that. We heard their mocking laughter along with the splash. "Bye, girls!" Silvia shouted triumphantly as she set off swimming, and we were frozen there in spite of the heat—weird, we were frozen and more boiling hot than ever, our ears burning in shame as we cast about desperately for a comeback and watched them glide away, laughing at the dummies who didn't know how to swim. Humiliated, fifty yards away from the Virgin that now no one felt like looking at, that none of us had ever really wanted to see. We looked at Natalia. She was so filled with rage that the tears wouldn't fall from her eyes. We told her we should go back. She said no, she wanted to see the Virgin. We were tired and ashamed, and we sat down to smoke, saying we would wait for her.

She took a long time, about fifteen minutes. Strange—was she praying? We didn't ask her, we knew very well how she was when she got mad. Once, she'd bitten one of us in an attack of rage, for real, she left a giant bite mark on the arm that had stayed there for almost a week. Finally she came back, asked us for a drag—she didn't like to smoke whole cigarettes—and started to walk. We followed her. We could see Silvia and Diego on the beach, drying each other off. We couldn't hear them well, but they were laughing, and suddenly a shout from Silvia, "Don't get mad, girls, it was just a joke."

Natalia whirled around to face us. She was covered in dust. There was even dust in her eyes. She stared at us, studying us. Then she smiled and said:

"It's not a Virgin."

"What?"

"It has a white sheet to hide it, to cover it, but it's not a Virgin. It's a red woman made of plaster, and she's naked. She has black nipples."

We were scared. We asked her who it was, then. Natalia

said she didn't know, it must be a Brazilian thing. She also said she'd asked it for a favor. And that the red was really well painted, and it shone, like acrylic. That the statue had very pretty hair, long and black, darker and silkier than Silvia's. And when she approached it, the false virginal white fell on its own, she didn't touch it, like the statue wanted Natalia to see it. Then she'd asked it for something.

We didn't reply. Sometimes she did crazy things like that, like the menstrual blood in the coffee. Then she'd get over it.

We reached the beach in a very bad mood, and we ignored all of Silvia and Diego's attempts to make us laugh. We saw them start to feel guilty. They said they were sorry, asked our forgiveness. They admitted it had been a bad joke, mean, designed to embarrass us, mean and condescending. They opened the little cooler we always brought to the quarry and took out a cold beer, and just as Diego flipped off the cap with his keychain-opener, we heard the first growl. It was so loud, clear, and strong that it seemed to come from very close by. But Silvia stood up and pointed to the hill where the owner supposedly could appear. It was a black dog, though the first thing Diego said was, "It's a horse." No sooner did he finish the word, the dog barked, and the bark filled the afternoon and we could have sworn it made the surface of the water in the quarry pool tremble a little. It was big as a pony, completely black, and it was clearly about to come down the hill. But it wasn't the only one. The first growl had come from behind us, at the end of the beach. There, very close to us, three slobbering pony-dogs were walking. You could see their ribs as their sides rose and fell—they were skinny. These were not the owner's dogs, we thought, they were the

dogs the bus driver had told us about, savage and dangerous. Diego made a "shhh" sound to soothe them, and Silvia
said, "We can't show them we're scared." And then Natalia,
furious, finally crying now, screamed at them: "You arrogant
assholes, you're a flat-ass skank, and you're a shithead, and
those are my dogs!"

There was one ten feet away from Silvia. Diego didn't
even hear Natalia: he stood in front of his girlfriend to pro-
tect her, but then another dog appeared behind him, and
then two smaller ones that came running and barking down
the hill where the owner never did turn up, and suddenly
they started howling, from hunger or hatred, we didn't know.
What we did know, what we realized because it was so obvi-
ous, was that the dogs didn't even look at us. None of us.
They ignored us, it was like we didn't exist, like it was only
Silvia and Diego there beside the quarry pool. Natalia put on
a shirt and a skirt, whispered to us to get dressed too, and
then she took us by the hands. She walked to the iron arch
over the entranceway that led to the highway, and only then
did she start to run to the 307 stop; we followed her. If we
thought about getting help, we didn't say anything. If we
thought about going back, we didn't mention that either.
When we got to the highway and heard Silvia's and Diego's
screams, we secretly prayed that no car would stop and hear
them too; sometimes, since we were so young and pretty, people stopped and offered to take us to the city for free. The 307
came and we got on calmly so as not to raise suspicions. The
driver asked us how we were and we told him, fine, great, it's
all good, it's all good.

The Cart

Juancho was drunk that day. He was getting belligerent as he walked up and down the sidewalk, although by that point no one in the neighborhood felt threatened, or even unsettled, by his drunken antics. Halfway down the block, Horacio was washing his car like he did every Sunday, in shorts and flip-flops, his prominent belly taut, his chest hair white, the radio tuned to the game. On the corner, the Spaniards from the variety store were drinking *mate* with the kettle on the ground between the two folding recliners they'd brought outside because the sun was nice. Across the way, Coca's boys were drinking beer in the doorway, and a group of girls, freshly bathed and overly made-up, were chatting as they stood in the doorway of Valeria's garage. Earlier, my dad had tried to say hi and start a conversation with the neighbors, but he came back inside as always, downcast, a little annoyed, because he was a good guy but he didn't know small talk—he said the same things every Sunday afternoon.

My mom was spying out the window. She got bored with the Sunday TV, but she didn't feel like going out. She peered between the half-open blinds, and would occasionally ask us to bring her a cup of tea, or a cookie, or an aspirin. My brother and I usually spent Sundays at home; sometimes, at night, we'd take a spin downtown if Dad would lend us the car.

Mom saw him first. He was coming from the direction of Tuyutí's corner, walking in the middle of the street and pushing a loaded-down supermarket cart. He was even drunker than Juancho, but somehow he managed to push that pile of garbage in the cart—all bottles, cardboard, and phone books. He stopped in front of Horacio's car, swaying. It was hot that day, but the man was wearing an old, greenish pullover. He must have been around sixty years old. He left the cart at the curb, went over to the car, and, right on the side where my mother had the best view, he pulled down his pants.

She called to us to come see. We came to the window and all three of us peered through the blinds with her: my brother, my dad, and me. The man, who wasn't wearing underwear under his filthy dress pants, shat on the sidewalk: soft shit, almost diarrhea, and a lot of it. The smell reached us, and it stank as much of alcohol as it did of shit.

"Poor man," said my mom.

"A person can come to such misery," said my dad.

Horacio was stupefied, but you could tell he was about to

get mad, because his neck was turning red. But before he could react, Juancho ran across the street and pushed the man, who hadn't even had time to stand up, or pull up his pants. The old man fell into his own shit, which spattered onto his sweater and his right hand. He only murmured an "Oh."

"Black-ass bum!" Juancho shouted at him. "You vagrant son of a bitch, how dare you come here and shit on our neighborhood, you uppity cocksucking scumbag!"

He kicked the man on the ground. Juancho was wearing flip-flops, and his feet also got spattered with shit.

"Get up, you bastard, you get up and hose down Horacio's sidewalk—you can't fuck around here—and then get back to whatever slum you crawled out of, you son of a motherfucking bitch."

And he went on kicking the man, in the chest, in the back. The man couldn't get up; he seemed not to understand what was happening. Suddenly he started to cry.

"It's not worth all that," said my dad.

"How can he humiliate the poor man like that?" said my mom, and she stood up and headed for the door. We followed her. When Mom got to the sidewalk, Juancho had gotten the man up, whimpering and apologizing, and was trying to shove into his hands the hose Horacio had been using to wash the car, so he could wash away his own shit. The whole block stank. No one dared approach. Horacio said, "Juancho, leave it," but in a low voice.

My mom intervened. Everyone respected her, especially Juancho, because she would give him a few coins for wine when he asked her. The others treated her with deference because though Mom was a physical therapist, everyone thought she was a doctor, and that's what they all called her.

"Leave him alone. Let him go, it's fine. We'll clean up. He's drunk, he doesn't know what he's doing, there's no cause to hit him."

The old man looked at Mom, and she told him, "Sir, apologize and be on your way." He murmured something, dropped the hose, and, still with his pants down, tried to push the cart away.

"The doctor saved your life, you asshole, but the cart stays here. You pay for your filth, dirty-ass trespasser, you don't fuck around in this neighborhood."

Mom tried to dissuade Juancho, but he was drunk, and furious, and he was shouting like a vigilante, and there was nothing white left in his eyes, only black and red, the same colors as the shorts he was wearing. He stood in front of the cart and he wouldn't let the man push it. I was afraid another fight would break out—another pounding from Juancho, really—but the man seemed to give up. He zipped up his pants—they didn't have a button—and walked off, in the middle of the street again, toward Catamarca; everyone watched him go, the Spaniards murmuring *how awful*, Coca's boys cackling, some of the girls in Valeria's garage laughing nervously, others with their heads down, as though ashamed. Horacio cursed under his breath. Juancho took a bottle from the cart and threw it at the man, but it missed him by a long shot and shattered against the concrete. The man, startled by the noise, turned around and shouted something unintelligible. We didn't know if he was speaking another language (but which?), or if he was simply too drunk to articulate. But before running off in a zigzag, fleeing from Juancho, who was chasing him and shouting, he looked straight at my mom, fully lucid, and nodded twice. He said something else, rolling his eyes, taking in the whole block and more. Then he disappeared around the corner. Juancho was too wasted to follow. He just went on yelling for a long time.

Everyone went inside. The neighbors would go on talking about the episode all afternoon, and all week long. Horacio used the hose, all grumbling and "Fucking bums, fucking bums."

"What can you expect from this neighborhood," said Mom, and she closed the blinds.

Someone, probably Juancho himself, moved the cart to Tuyutí's corner and left it parked in front of the house Doña Rita had left empty when she died the year before. After a few days, no one payed it any attention. At first they did, because they expected the *villero*—what else could he be but a slum-dweller?—to come back for it. But he never turned up, and no one knew what to do with his things. So there they stayed, and one day they got wet in the rain, and the damp cardboard disintegrated and gave off a smell. Something else stank amid all the junk, probably rotting food, but disgust kept people from cleaning. It was enough to give the cart a wide berth, walk real close to the houses and not look at it. There were always gross smells in the neighborhood, coming from the greenish muck that flowed along the gutters, or from the Riachuelo when a certain breeze blew, especially at dusk.

It all started around fifteen days after the cart arrived. Maybe it started before that, but there had to be an accumulation of misfortune for the neighborhood to feel like something strange was going on. Horacio was the first. He had a rotisserie downtown, and it did well. One night, when he was balancing the register, some thieves came in and took it all. These things happen. But that same night, after filing the report—useless, as in most robberies, among other reasons because the thugs wore masks—when Horacio went to the ATM to take out money, he found out he didn't have a single peso in his account. He called the bank, made a fuss, kicked in doors, tried to throat punch an employee, and he took things to the branch manager, and then to the regional manager. But there was nothing for it: the money wasn't there, someone had taken it out, and Horacio, from one day to the next, was ruined. He sold his car. He got less for it than he expected.

Coca's two boys lost the jobs they had in the auto repair shop on the avenue. Without warning; the owner didn't even give them explanations. They yelled and cursed at him, and he kicked them out. Then, to top it off, Coca's pension didn't come through. Her sons spent a week looking for work, and after that they set to squandering their savings on beer. Coca got into bed saying she wanted to die. No one would give them credit anywhere. They didn't even have bus fare.

The Spaniards had to close the variety store. Because it wasn't just Coca's boys, or Horacio; every one of the neighbors, all of a sudden, in a matter of days, lost everything. The merchandise at the kiosk disappeared mysteriously. The taxi driver's car was stolen. Mari's husband and only support, a bricklayer, fell off a scaffold and died. The girls had to leave their private schools because their parents couldn't afford them; the dentist had no more clients, neither did the dressmaker, and a short-circuit blew out all the butcher's freezers.

After two months no one in the neighborhood had a phone anymore—they couldn't afford it. After three months, they had to tap the electricity wires because they couldn't pay their bills. Coca's boys went out to pickpocket and one of them, the most inept, got caught by the police. Then one night the other one didn't come home; maybe he'd been killed. The taxi driver ventured on foot to the other side of the avenue. There, he said, everything was fine as could be. Up to three months after it all started, businesses on the other side of the avenue gave credit. But eventually, they stopped.

Horacio put his house up for sale.

Everyone locked their houses with old chains, because there was no money for alarms or more effective locks; things started to go missing from houses, TVs and radios and stereos and computers, and you'd see some neighbors lugging appliances between two or three of them, hoisted in their arms or loaded into shopping carts. They took it all to pawnshops and used-appliance stores across the avenue. But other neighbors organized, and when the thieves tried to knock down their doors, they brandished knives, or guns if they had them. Cholo, the vegetable vender around the corner, cracked the taxi driver's skull with the iron he used for grilling. At first, a group of women organized to ration out the food that was left in the freezers, but when they discovered that some people lied and kept supplies for themselves, the goodwill went all to hell.

Coca ate her cat, and then she killed herself. Someone had to go to the Social Services office on the avenue for them to take away the body and bury it for free. One of the employees there wanted to find out more, and the neighbors told him, and then the TV cameras came to record the localized bad luck that was sinking three blocks of the neighborhood into misery. They especially wanted to know why the neighbors farther away, the ones who lived four blocks over, for example, didn't show solidarity.

Social workers came and handed out food, but that only led to more wars breaking out. At five months, not even the police would come in, and the people who still went to watch TV on the display sets in the appliance stores on the avenue said that the news talked of nothing else. But soon the neighbors were totally isolated, because when the people on the avenue recognized them, they were shooed away.

The neighbors were isolated, I say, because we did have TV, and electricity, and gas, and a phone. We said we didn't, and we lived as battened down as the rest; if we met someone on the street, we lied: we ate the dog, we ate the plants, Diego—my brother—got credit at a store twenty blocks from here. My mom managed things so she could go out to work, jumping from roof to roof (it wasn't so hard in a neighborhood where all the houses were low). My dad could take out his pension from an ATM, and we paid our services online, because we still had internet. No one sacked our house; respect for the doctor, maybe, or very good acting on our part.

One day, Juancho was sitting on the sidewalk drinking wine straight from the bottle that he'd stolen from a distant supermarket. He was the one who started to yell and curse:

"It's the fucking cart, the *villero*'s cart." He yelled for hours, spent hours walking the street, banging on doors and windows: "It's the cart, it's the old man's fault, we have to go find him, let's go, you pieces of shit, he put some kind of macumba curse on us." Juancho's hunger showed more than the others' because he'd never had anything before, he lived off the coins he collected every day, ringing doorbells (people always gave him something, out of fear or compassion, who knows). That same night he set the cart on fire, and the neighbors watched the flames out their windows. And Juancho was right about something. Everyone had thought it was the cart. Something in it. Something contagious it had brought from the slum.

That same night, my dad gathered us into the dining room for a family meeting. He told us that we had to leave. That people were going to realize we were immune. That Mari, the next-door neighbor, already suspected something, because it was pretty hard to hide the smell of food, even though when we cooked we took care to seal the openings around the door so the smoke and the smells didn't waft out. Our luck was going to run out; everything went bad. Mom agreed. She told us she'd been spotted jumping over the back roof. She couldn't be sure, but she'd felt eyes on her. Diego too. He said that one day, when he raised the blinds, he'd seen some neighbors running away, but others had stayed and stared at him, defiant; bad ones, crazy by now. Almost no one saw us, we stayed locked in the house, but to keep up the charade we would have to go out soon. And we weren't skinny or gaunt. We were scared, but fear doesn't look the same as desperation.

We listened to Dad's plan, which didn't seem very reasonable. Mom told us hers, and it was a little better, but nothing out of this world. We all agreed on Diego's: my brother's way of thinking was always more simple and matter-of-fact.

We went to bed, but none of us could sleep. After tossing and turning, I knocked on my brother's door. I found him sitting on the floor. He was really pale from lack of sun—we all were. I asked him if he thought Juancho was right. He nodded.

"Mom saved us. Did you see how the man looked at her, before he left? She saved us."

"So far," I said.

"So far," he said.

That night, we smelled burnt meat. Mom was in the kitchen and we went in to reprimand her—was she crazy, putting a steak on the grill at that hour? People were going to catch on. But Mom was trembling beside the counter.

"That's not regular meat," she said.

We opened the blinds a crack and looked up. We saw the smoke coming from the terrace across from us. And it was black, and it didn't smell like any other smoke we knew.

"Damn old ghetto son of a bitch," said Mom, and she started to cry.

The Well

I am terrified by this dark thing
That sleeps in me;
All day I feel its soft, feathery turnings, its malignity.

SYLVIA PLATH, "ELM"

Josefina remembered the trip—the heat, the crowded Renault 12—like it was just a few days ago, and not back when she was six, just after Christmas, under the stifling January sun. Her father drove, barely speaking; her mother was in the passenger seat and Josefina was in back, stuck between her sister and her grandma Rita, who was peeling mandarins and flooding the car with the smell of overheated fruit. They were going to Corrientes on vacation, to visit her aunt and uncle on her mother's side, but that was only part of the larger reason for the trip, which Josefina couldn't even guess at. No one spoke much, she remembered. Her grandmother and her mother both wore dark glasses, and they only opened their mouths to warn of a truck passing too close to the car, or to beg her father to slow down; they were tense and alert and waiting for an accident.

They were afraid. They were always afraid. In summer, when Josefina and Mariela wanted to swim in the above-ground pool, Grandma Rita filled it with five inches of water, and then sat in a chair in the shade of the patio's lemon tree to keep watch over every splash, so she'd be sure to get there in time if her granddaughters started to drown. Josefina remembered how her mother used to cry and call in doctors and ambulances at dawn if she or her sister had a fever of just a couple degrees. Or how she made them miss school for a harmless cold. She never let them sleep over at their friends' houses, and she hardly ever let them play on the sidewalk; when she did, they could see her keeping watch over them from the window, hidden behind the curtains. Sometimes Mariela cried at night, saying that something was moving under her bed, and she could never sleep with the light off. Josefina was the only one of the family's women who was never afraid; she was like her father. Until that trip to Corrientes.

She couldn't remember how many days they had spent at her aunt and uncle's house, nor if they had gone to the waterfront or to window-shop on the pedestrian walkways. But she remembered the visit to Doña Irene's house perfectly. The sky had been cloudy that day but the heat was heavy, as always in Corrientes before a storm. Her father hadn't gone with them; Doña Irene's house was near her aunt and uncle's, and the four of them had walked there with her aunt Clarita. They didn't call Irene a witch; mostly they just called her The Woman. Her house had a beautiful front yard, a little overfull of plants, and almost right in the center there was a white-painted well. When Josefina saw it, she let go of her grandmother's hand and ran, ignoring the howls of panic, to get a closer look and peer in over the edge. They couldn't stop her until she saw the bottom of the well and the stagnant water in its depths.

Her mother gave her a slap that could well have made Josefina cry, except that she was used to those nervous wallops that ended in sobs and hugs and "My baby, my baby, if anything ever happened to you." Like what? Josefina had thought. She'd never considered jumping into the well. No one was going to push her. She just wanted to see if the water would reflect her face the way wells always did in fairy tales—her face like a blond-haired moon in the black water.

Josefina had fun that afternoon at The Woman's house. Her mother, grandmother, and sister, sitting on stools, had let Josefina nose around among the offerings and knickknacks piled up in front of an altar; Aunt Clarita waited discreetly outside in the yard, smoking. The Woman talked, or prayed, but Josefina didn't remember anything strange—no chanting, no clouds of smoke, no placing of hands on her family. The Woman just whispered to them low enough that Josefina couldn't hear what she was saying, but she didn't care. On the altar she found baby booties, fresh and dried bouquets of flowers, photographs in color and black-and-white, crosses adorned with red cords, a lot of rosaries—plastic, wood, silver-plated metal. There was also the ugly figure of the saint her grandmother prayed to, San La Muerte, Saint Death—a skeleton with its scythe. The figure was repeated in different sizes and materials, sometimes in rough approximations, others carved in detail, with deep black eye sockets and a broad grin.

After a while Josefina got bored and The Woman told her, "Little one, why don't you rest in the armchair, go on now." She did, and she fell asleep immediately, sitting up. When she woke it was nighttime, and Aunt Clarita had gotten tired of waiting for them. They had to walk back on their own. Josefina remembered how, before they left, she'd tried to go back and look into the well, but she couldn't bring herself to do it. It was dark and the white paint shone like the bones of San La Muerte; it was the first time she felt fear. They returned to Buenos Aires a few days later. That first night back in their house, Josefina hadn't been able to sleep when Mariela turned off the light.

Mariela slept soundly in the little bed across from her, and now the night-light was on Josefina's bedside table; she didn't feel tired until the glowing hands of the Hello Kitty clock showed three or four in the morning. Mariela would be hugging a doll, and Josefina would watch its plastic eyes shine humanly in the half dark. Or she'd hear a rooster crow in the middle of the night and remember—but who had told her?—that at that hour of the night a rooster's crow was a sign that someone was going to die. And that had to mean her, so she took her own pulse—she'd learned how by watching her mother, who always checked the girls' heartbeats when they had a fever. If her pulse was too fast, she'd get so scared she wouldn't even dare call her parents to come and save her. If it was slow, she kept her hand against her chest to

be sure her heart didn't stop. Sometimes she fell asleep count-
ing, eyes on the second hand. One night, she discovered that
the blot of plaster on the ceiling just over her bed—a repair
after a leak—was shaped like a head with horns: the face of
the devil. That time she'd told Mariela, but her sister, laughing, said that stains were like clouds, you could see all kinds
of shapes if you looked at them too long. And Mariela didn't
see any devil; to her it looked like a bird on two legs. One
night Josefina heard the neighing of a horse or donkey and
her hands started to sweat at the thought that it had to be the
Mule Spirit, the ghost of a dead woman who'd been turned
into a mule and couldn't rest, and who went out to gallop at
night. That one she'd told her father; he'd kissed her head
and told her those stories were rubbish, and that afternoon
she'd heard him yelling at her mother: "Tell her to stop feeding the girl all that bullshit! I don't want your mother filling
up her head with those superstitions, the ignorant old bag!"
Her grandmother denied telling her any stories, and she
wasn't lying. Josefina had no clue where she'd gotten those
ideas, she just felt like she knew, the same way she knew she
couldn't put her hand to a hot stove without burning herself,
or that in the fall she needed to wear a jacket over her shirt
because it got cool in the evenings.

Years later, sitting across from one of her many psychologists, she had tried to explain and rationalize her fears one by
one: what Mariela said about the plaster could be true, and
maybe she *had* heard her grandmother tell those stories, they
were part of the Corrientes mythology, and maybe one of the
neighbors had a chicken coop, maybe the mule belonged to
the junk sellers who lived around the corner. But she didn't

believe any of those explanations. Her mother would go to the sessions too, and explain how she and her own mother were "anxious" and "phobic" and they certainly could have passed on those fears to Josefina; but they were recovering, and Mariela no longer suffered from night terrors, and so "Jose's issue" was surely just a matter of time.

But time dragged on for years, and Josefina hated her father because one day he took off and left her alone with those women who, after years of hiding away inside, now planned vacations and weekend outings, while Josefina felt faint when she reached the front door; she hated that she'd had to leave school, and that her mother had to take her at the end of the year to sit for exams; she hated that the only kids who visited her house were Mariela's friends; she hated how they talked about "Jose's issue" in quiet voices, and above all she hated spending days in her room reading stories that at night turned into nightmares. She'd read the story of Anahí and the ceibo flower, and in her dreams a woman had appeared wrapped in flames; she'd read about the potoo bird, and now before she fell asleep she would hear its call, which was really the voice of a dead girl crying near her window. She couldn't go to La Boca because it seemed to her that the river's black surface hid submerged bodies that would surely try to rise up as soon as she got near its edge. She never slept with a leg uncovered, because she just knew she would feel a cold hand touching it. Josefina's mother left her with Grandma Rita when she had to go out; if she was half an hour late Josefina would start to vomit, because the delay could mean only that her mother had died in a car crash. She ran past the portrait of the dead grandfather she'd never met—she could feel his black eyes following her—and she never went near the room that held her mother's old piano, because she *knew* that when no one else was playing it, the devil took a turn.

From the sofa, her hair so greasy it always looked wet, Josefina watched the world she was missing go by. She hadn't even attended her sister's fifteenth birthday party, and she knew Mariela was grateful. She went from one psychiatrist to another for years, and certain pills had allowed her to go back to school, but only until the third year, when she'd discovered that there were other voices in the school's hallways, beneath the hum of kids planning parties and benders. Then there was the time she'd been in a bathroom stall and seen bare feet walking over the tiles, and a classmate told her it must be the suicidal nun who'd hung herself from the flagpole years before. It was useless for her mother and the principal and the school counselor to tell her that no nun had ever killed herself in the schoolyard; Josefina was already having nightmares about the Sacred Heart of Jesus, Christ's open chest that bled and drenched her face in blood, about Lazarus, pale and rotting as he rose from a tomb among the rocks, and about angels that tried to rape her.

And so she'd stayed home, and went back to taking exams at the end of each year with a doctor's excuse. Meanwhile, Mariela was coming home at dawn in cars that screeched to a halt in front of the house, and she heard the kids' shouts at the end of a night of adventure that Josefina couldn't even begin to imagine. She envied Mariela even when her mother was yelling at her about a phone bill that was impossible to pay; if only Josefina had someone to talk to. Because her group therapy sessions sure didn't work; all those kids with real problems—absent parents or violent childhoods—who talked about drugs and sex and anorexia and heartbreak. But she kept going anyway, always in a taxi there and back—and the taxi driver always had to be the same one, and he had to wait for her at the door because she got dizzy and her pounding heart wouldn't let her breathe if she was ever left alone in the street. She hadn't gotten on a bus since that trip to Corrientes, and the only time she'd been in the subway she had screamed until she lost her voice, and her mother had to get her out at the next stop. That time, her mother had shaken her and dragged her up the stairs, but Josefina didn't care, she just had to get out of that confinement any way possible, away from the noise and that snaking darkness.

The new pills—sky blue, practically experimental, shiny like they'd just come from the lab—went down easy, and in just a little while they managed to make the sidewalk seem less like a minefield. They even let her sleep without dreams she could remember, and when she turned out the bedside lamp one night, she didn't feel the sheets grow cold as a tomb. She was still afraid, but she could go to the newsstand alone without the certainty she would die on the way. Mariela seemed more pleased than Josefina was. She suggested they get coffee together, and Josefina got up the nerve to go—in a taxi there and back, of course. That afternoon she'd been able to talk to her sister like never before, and she surprised herself by making plans to go to the movies (Mariela promised to leave halfway through if necessary), and even confessing that maybe she wanted to go to college, as long as there weren't too many people in the classrooms and she could stay close to the doors or windows. Mariela hugged her unabashedly, and when she did she knocked one of the mugs to the floor, where it broke right in half. The waiter picked up the pieces with a smile; and why wouldn't he? Mariela was so beautiful, with her wispy blond hair hanging over her face, her full lips always damp, and her eyes lightly lined in black so the green of her irises would hypnotize all who looked at her.

They went out several more times for coffee—they never made it to the movies—and one of those afternoons Mariela brought along the brochures for different majors she thought might appeal to Josefina: anthropology, sociology, literature. But she seemed jittery, and it wasn't the same nervousness of their first outings, when she'd had to be prepared to call an emergency taxi—or, in the worst case, an ambulance—to bring Josefina back home or to the hospital. She pushed her long blond hair behind her ears and lit a cigarette.

"Jose," she said. "There's something else."

"What?"

"Do you remember when we went to Corrientes? You must have been six years old, I was eight . . ."

"Yes."

"Well, do you remember that we went to a witch? Mom and Grandma wanted to go because they were like you, they were afraid all the time, and they wanted her to cure them."

Josefina was now listening intently. Her heart was pounding fast, but she breathed deeply, dried her hands on her pants, and tried to concentrate on what her sister was saying, like her psychiatrist had advised her to do: "When the fear comes," she'd said, "pay attention to something else. Anything else. Look at what the person next to you is reading. Read billboards, or count how many red cars go by in the street."

"And I remember the witch said they could go back if it happened to them again. Maybe you could go. Now that you're better. I know it's crazy, I'm as bad as Grandma with her small-town superstitious bullshit. But they got over it, right?"

"Mariela, I can't travel. You know I can't."

"What if I go with you? I can do it, seriously. We'll plan it really well."

"No way. I can't."

"Okay. Well, think about it. What do I know? But I'll help you, for real."

The morning she tried to leave the house to go register for college, Josefina found that the stretch between the door and the taxi was insurmountable. Before she could put one foot on the sidewalk, her knees were trembling, and she was already crying. It had been several days since she'd first noticed a stalling and even a reversal in the pills' effect. She'd gone back to feeling it was impossible to fill up her lungs, or more like she paid obsessive attention to every inhalation, as if she had to oversee the entrance of air for the system to work, as if she were giving herself mouth-to-mouth resuscitation just to stay alive. Once again she was paralyzed at the slightest change in the placement of objects in her room;

once again she had to turn on the bedside light before she could sleep, and now also the TV and the ceiling lamp, because she couldn't bear a single shadow. She expected every symptom—she recognized them as they appeared—but for the first time she felt something else beneath the resignation and despair. She was angry. She was also exhausted, but she didn't want to go back to bed and try to control her shaking and her pounding heart, or drag herself to the sofa in pajamas to imagine the rest of her life, a future of psychiatric hospitals or private nurses. Because she couldn't resort to suicide—she was so afraid of dying!

But she did start thinking about Corrientes and The Woman. And about what life had been like in her house before that trip. She remembered her grandmother crying and kneeling beside the bed to pray the storm would stop, because she was afraid of the flashing lightning, the thunder, even the rain. She remembered how her mother stared out the window with wide eyes every time the street flooded, and how she shouted that they were all going to drown if the water didn't stop rising. She remembered how Mariela had never wanted to go out and play with the neighborhood kids, not even when they came over to get her, how she'd hugged her dolls as if afraid someone would steal them. She remembered how once a week her father had taken her mother to the psychiatrist, and how she always came back half-asleep and went straight to bed. And she even remembered Doña Carmen, who'd taken care of running errands and cashing pension checks for her grandmother, who didn't want to— who *couldn't*, Josefina now knew—leave the house. Doña Carmen had been dead for ten years now, two more than her grandmother, and after the trip to Corrientes she'd only come over for tea, because all the isolation and terror had ended. For them. Because, for Josefina, they were just beginning.

What had happened in Corrientes? Had The Woman forgotten to "cure" her? But there'd been no need to cure her of anything, because Josefina wasn't afraid. But then, a little while later when she'd begun to suffer from the same thing as the others, why hadn't they taken her back to The Woman? Didn't they love her? And what if Mariela was wrong? Josefina began to understand that her anger was the end, that if she didn't hold on to the anger and let it carry her to a long-distance bus, to The Woman, she would never come out of that isolation, and that it was worth dying to try.

She waited up one dawn for Mariela, and made her a cup of coffee to clear her head.

"Mariela, let's go. I want to do it."

"Where?"

Josefina was afraid her sister would back out, withdraw her offer, but then she realized Mariela was slow to understand because she was a little drunk. "To Corrientes, to see the witch."

Mariela looked at her, suddenly completely lucid.

"Are you sure?"

"I thought about it. I'll take a lot of pills and sleep the whole way there. If things go bad . . . you give me more. They don't do anything. Worst case, I'll sleep a whole lot."

Josefina boarded the bus practically asleep; she'd waited for it sitting next to her sister on a bench, snoring, her head resting on her bag. Mariela had looked frightened when she saw her take five pills with a sip of 7UP, but she didn't say anything. And it worked, because Josefina woke up at the Corrientes terminal, an acid taste filling her mouth and her head pounding. Her sister hugged her during the entire taxi ride to their aunt and uncle's house, and Josefina tried to stop her teeth from chattering so hard she thought they'd break. She went straight to Aunt Clarita's bedroom—their aunt was expecting them—and she wouldn't accept food or drink or visits from relatives. She could barely open her mouth to swallow the pills, her jaws hurt, and she couldn't forget the flash of malice and panic in her mother's eyes when she'd told her she was going to look for the witch, or how she'd said, "You know full well it's pointless," in a triumphant voice. Mariela had shouted at her, "You evil goddamn bitch," and wouldn't listen to any reasoning. Locked in the room with Josefina, she stayed awake all night without a word, smoking and picking out light pants and shirts for the Corrientes heat. Josefina was already drugged when they left for the terminal, but she was conscious enough to notice that her mother hadn't come out of her room to see them off.

Aunt Clarita told them The Woman was still living in the same house, but she was very old and didn't attend the public anymore. Mariela insisted: they'd come to Corrientes just to see her, and they weren't going to leave until they did. The fear in Clarita's eyes was the same one she'd seen in her mother's, Josefina realized. And she also understood her aunt wasn't going to go with them, so she squeezed Mariela's arm to interrupt her shouting ("But what the hell is wrong with you? Why won't you help either? Just look at her!") and she whispered, "Let's go alone." For the three blocks to The Woman's house—which felt like miles—Josefina thought about that "Just look at her," and she got angry at her sister. Josefina could be pretty too if her hair weren't falling out, if she didn't have those patches above her forehead where her scalp showed through; she could have those long, strong legs if she were capable of walking at least around the block; she would know how to put on makeup if she had somewhere to go and someone to go with; her hands would be beautiful if she didn't chew her nails down to the cuticles; her skin would be golden like Mariela's if the sun touched it more often. And her eyes wouldn't always be red and sunken if she could only sleep, or distract herself with something other than TV and the internet.

Mariela had to clap her hands in The Woman's front yard to get her to come to the door, because the house didn't have a doorbell. Josefina looked at the garden, more overgrown now, the roses dying from heat, the lilies drooping, rue plants everywhere grown to incredible heights. The Woman appeared on the threshold just when Josefina spotted the well, nearly hidden among the weeds, its white paint peeling to reveal the red brick underneath.

The Woman recognized them right away and ushered them in. It was as if she'd been waiting for them. The altar was still standing, but it had triple the offerings now, and a giant San La Muerte the size of a church crucifix; lights flashed intermittently inside its eye sockets, surely from a strand of electric Christmas lights. The Woman wanted to sit Josefina in the same armchair where she'd slept almost twenty years before, but she had to run to get a bucket because the retching had started. Josefina vomited up stomach fluids and she felt like her heart was blocking her throat, but then The Woman put a hand on her forehead.

"Breathe deeply, little one, breathe."

Josefina did as she was told, and for the first time in many years she felt the relief of lungs full of air, free, no longer trapped behind her ribs. She felt like crying, like giving thanks; she was certain that The Woman was curing her. But when she raised her head to look her in the eyes, trying to smile with her jaws clenched tight, she saw sorrow and remorse on The Woman's face.

"My child, it's no use. When they brought you here, it was done. I had to throw it down the well. I knew the saints would never forgive me, I knew Añá would bring you back."

Josefina shook her head. She was feeling better. What was the witch trying to tell her? Was she really old and crazy like Aunt Clarita had said? But The Woman stood up with a sigh, went over to the altar, and brought back an old photograph. She recognized it: her mother and her grandmother, sitting on either end of a sofa, and between them Mariela on the right and an empty space on the left, where Josefina should have been.

"I felt bad for them, so bad. All three of them with evil thoughts, gooseflesh, the damage of many years. I was out of my skin just looking at them, I was heaving; I couldn't take that evil out of them."

"What evil?"

"Old evil, child, evil that can't be spoken," The Woman made the sign of the cross. "Not even Christ of the Two Lights could defeat it, no. It was old. They were under attack.

But you, child, were not. It didn't attack you. I don't know why."

"*What* didn't attack me?"

"Evils! They cannot be spoken." The Woman brought a finger to her lips, asking for silence, and she closed her eyes. "I couldn't take the rotten part out of them and put it in me because I didn't have that kind of strength; no one does. I couldn't make it flow out, I couldn't clean it. I could only pass it on, and I did. I passed it to you, child, while you were sleeping there. San La Muerte said he wouldn't hurt you as much, because you were pure. But the saint lied to me, or I misunderstood him. Those three wanted to pass it on to you, and they said they would take care of you. But they didn't take care of you. And I had to throw it away. The photo, I threw it into the well. But we can't get it back. I can't ever take the evil out of you, because the evil is in your picture, in the water, and the photo has rotted away by now. The evils stayed there in your picture, stuck to you."

The Woman covered her face with her hands. Josefina thought she saw Mariela crying, but she ignored her, trying to understand.

"They wanted to save themselves, child. This one too," and she waved toward Mariela. "She was green, but already mean."

Josefina stood up with what was left of the air in her lungs, with the new strength that fortified her legs. It wasn't going to last long, she was sure, but please, let it be enough, enough to run to the well and throw myself into the rainwater, and please let it be bottomless so I can drown there with the photo and the betrayal. The Woman and Mariela didn't follow her, and Josefina ran as fast as she could but when she reached the edge of the well her wet hands slipped, her knees grew stiff, and she couldn't, she couldn't climb up, and she barely managed to see the reflection of her face in the water before she collapsed to sit among the overgrown weeds, crying, choking, because she was so, so very afraid to jump.

Rambla Triste

It was possible that her stuffy nose—she always caught a cold on planes—was distorting her sense of smell; that had to be it, but once she blew her nose and could take in air, the smell got even worse. She didn't remember Barcelona being so dirty. At least, she hadn't noticed it on her first visit, five years ago. But it had to be a cold, maybe the stench of stagnant mucus, because for blocks at a time she smelled absolutely nothing, and then suddenly the odor attacked her and made her stomach heave violently. It smelled like a dead dog rotting beside the road, like rancid meat forgotten in the fridge and turned wine-purple. The smell would lie in wait, and then blasts of it would ruin the prettiest streets, the quaint alleys with clothes on lines from one balcony to another so you couldn't see the sky. It even reached the Ramblas. Sofía looked intently at the tourists to see if their noses were wrinkled like hers, but none of them were visibly disgusted. Maybe she was imagining it because she didn't like the city anymore. The narrow little streets that had seemed romantic before now made her feel afraid; the bars had lost their charm, and now reminded her of the ones in Buenos Aires, full of drunks who shouted or wanted to start up stupid conversations; the heat, which before had seemed so Mediterranean, dry and delicious, was now suffocating. But she didn't want to talk about these new impressions with her friends; she didn't want to be the typical haughty Argentine tourist superciliously pointing out all the defects of the paradise city.

She wanted to leave.

Maybe it was all because of the girl.

Five years earlier, Calle Escudellers had been packed end to end with junkies lying on the sidewalk on piles of their own dirty clothes. They weren't there anymore; they must have been driven out by the police, by fines and citations, not to mention the trucks that cleaned the city all night, spraying water on any spot where a person might sit innocently and drink a beer and eat a kebab. Now you had to keep walking or go into the bars; the street was only for movement. Walking the route she knew through Raval, she avoided creepy Calle Robadors—dark and full of criminals, said the legend perpetuated by its name, which no one dared discredit—and she came to Marquès de Barberà, wider and better lit. A girl was walking ahead of her, somewhat unstable, with jeans too low and tight on her hips so her flaccid belly spilled out from under her short shirt—a roll of chalky, stretch-marked flesh that would have been easy to hide with a long, baggy shirt, but the girl clearly wasn't worried about aesthetics. It was early, barely eight in the evening, but the street was oddly empty; not even the tourists from the hostel beside the internet café had come outside.

Suddenly the girl turned around, looked Sofía in the eyes, and said, with a thick Catalan accent but in very clear Spanish, "No puedo más." I just can't. Then, she pulled down her pants and defecated on the sidewalk, an explosive, painful diarrhea that made her scrunch up her face from the twisting cramps in her intestines. Then she collapsed against the wall. She missed falling into her own shit by a fraction of an inch.

Sofía tried to get her up, asked her where she lived, if she had a phone to call someone who could come and get her; she asked the girl what was wrong, what drugs she was on. But the girl only stared at her with frightened eyes, unable to speak. The smell was no longer imaginary and Sofía's eyes teared up as she fought back her gag reflex. Ten minutes later two policemen came and took the girl away; Sofía answered the officers' questions and stayed to be sure they treated her well, but she didn't stick around waiting for someone to clean the street. She lit a cigarette to banish the smell of shit, and she almost ran to Calle de la Cera, to Julieta's apartment, where she was going to spend those ten days in Barcelona. She used her own key to get in. The building's entrance was undergoing construction, because it had caught fire some months before. The lock on the front door didn't work well, and some vagrants had come inside to sleep; the fire they lit to ward off the cold had gotten out of hand.

Luckily, Julieta hadn't been in the apartment when it happened, but she'd also had her own problems with fire. Just a year before, in the middle of winter, she'd ended up in the hospital with carbon monoxide poisoning because the apartment's heater didn't have an exhaust to the outside.

The place where Julieta lived wasn't really an apartment: it was an office that was rented out as housing, without a bathroom, just a shared toilet and sink in the hallway outside. But it was large by Barcelona standards, cheap, and since it was a "penthouse," it had a balcony that was fantastic in summer. Sofía didn't know what Julieta had come to Spain looking for, but probably neither did Julieta. She'd been there eight years now, making animated shorts and videos for whoever hired her. When she got bored, she took unemployment. She got bored often.

She was making a salad when Sofía arrived. Julieta had become vegetarian as soon as she got to Europe, among other reasons because her first home was a squat where eating meat was considered a mortal sin. At first, she embraced her new friends' vegetarianism with militant passion. When she broke with them, disillusioned, she rejected the whole squatter lifestyle, except in the matter of nutrition. Sofía didn't mind sharing her host's diet; plus, she could always go downstairs to buy a delicious chicken or beef shawarma.

Sofía sat down on the red sofa that at night opened up to become a bed, and she told her friend about the girl and her diarrhea. Julieta tossed the salad and said that was normal for Barcelona.

"No other city in Spain has more crazy people. There aren't as many in Madrid, and even fewer in Zaragoza; my brother says not in Seville either. It's only here. Full of crazies on the loose, I don't know."

She served the salad onto two plates, sat at the table, and explained how that wasn't all: the crazies also came out in certain seasons. The hair-clip lady, for example. She was a woman who wore so many ornaments on her head you almost couldn't see her hair, and she only turned up in summer. The crazy guy with dreads, a fifty-something man who used a stick to bang on the metal shutters over closed businesses—he only showed up for the holidays, around Christmas. An awful racket, said Julieta; the banging sounded like gunshots and sometimes it sent the tourists running. She was used to it by now, but the first time she saw him she thought he was going to attack her, because in addition to banging with his stick, he yelled. And, she said, you'll get to see the old man from around the corner: he comes out in shifts, in the morning and afternoon, and he walks about fifty yards round-trip, sometimes shouting, sometimes grumbling softly, always waving his hands like he's trying to convince an invisible person of something very important. Julieta's theory was that his family made him go out for walks every day when they got sick of listening to him complain in the apartment, which, if it was on that block, had to be very small. The strange thing was that Julieta had never seen him come out of any door; she had to pay more attention, maybe, wait on the opposite sidewalk to figure out which house was his, mostly to shake off a strange feeling she got from the old madman. And not just that old madman, but all the crazy people in Barcelona who were concentrated in Raval.

"It's as if . . . What I'm about to say is insane. But what-ever. Sometimes I think the crazies aren't people, they're not real. They're like incarnations of the city's madness, like es-cape valves. If they weren't here, we'd all kill each other or die of stress, or, I don't know, we'd go after those asshole city guards who won't let you sit on the steps of the museum, or in the Plaza de los Àngels . . . have you seen them? The fuck-ers go on raids, and around here it's 'antisocial behavior' to sit on the sidewalk and drink a beer."

"They just started that!" The shout came from the bal-cony. It was Daniel, Julieta's boyfriend. He was also Argen-tine, but had been living in Barcelona for twelve years. Sofía hadn't realized he was home. Daniel came in, dried his hands on his pants, and started his diatribe. How when he got to Barcelona, the city was glorious. A lot of hard partying, maybe, but it was cool. Now it was a police city.

"Listen to this *garca* bullshit," he said, and he started to flip through a pile of newspapers until he found *La Vanguar-dia*. Sofía realized her friends made every effort not to speak the Spanish of Spain. They didn't call the apartment a "piso," but a "departamento"; they would never call anything sketchy "chungo"; something could be "malo," but never "mal rollo"; a mess was a "quilombo," never a "mogollón." She remembered how before, on her first visit, she'd laughed at how many "guapas" and "vengas" came out of the cou-ple's mouths. Now they seemed to have completely erased all local words, unless one slipped out by accident. It was surely intentional; a kind of Argentine fundamentalism, a mixture of nostalgia and genuine unease.

"Here it is, listen to this," Daniel said triumphantly, and he settled into the chair to read:

"The Plaza de los Àngels, when good weather arrives, recalls the Barcelona of two summers ago, when it bore the stigma of antisocial behavior. From nine o'clock at night on, countless bottles are scattered over the ramp and stairs in front of the MACBA, while a small army of vendors swarms the area hawking cans of beer. The efforts of the cleaning crews—more active and efficient than they were two years ago—still aren't enough to fully eliminate the piles of bottles, bags, and leftover food strewn over the pavement. Warm weather inspires a desire to enjoy the fresh air. Patronizing an outdoor terrace to drink a beer with friends after work seems appetizing, but there are those who would rather sit on the ground in the Plaza de los Àngels, the stage for an improvised street party. The young people arrive before dinner with drinks they've picked up in some nearby supermarket. But if they forget, they can always turn to the many vendors who offer beers for only a euro, much cheaper than in any local bar.

"One street vendor explained to this newspaper that he usually nets approximately thirty euros a night. The vendors set up schedules and territories so they don't compete. They buy cans for seventy cents and earn thirty selling them at a euro. They're taking a risk, because the public space ordinance sets fines of up to five hundred euros for the unauthorized sale of alcohol, in addition to possibly suffering the loss of unsold merchandise. Those who buy from these vendors are also taking a risk.

"That's how we live, with this snitchy journalism and in the middle of all this shit," huffed Daniel. "The other day they slapped a fine on a guy who was drinking a Coke in a plaza. They charged him like two hundred euros because he didn't want to get up when they went to hose the place down. They spray water all the time. And now you can't smoke in bars. Yeah, I know that's happening everywhere, but a bar isn't supposed to be a healthy place, goddammit. It's a place you go to scheme, to relax, to get wasted. But not here. The rents are scandalous: they only want rich people to live in this city, no one else. It's for tourists. They're cleaning the graffiti! There were some that were really beautiful, no other city in the world had graffiti like Barcelona's. But just try to explain to those brutes what art is. The fuck. They ruin everything."

"A friend of ours was arrested because he painted a slogan that said, 'Tourists, you're the terrorists.' They gave him like four months. Poor guy," said Julieta.

"You don't even know how bad we want to go to Madrid. But we have work here. I'm sick of this city. I don't even go out. I'd rather be bitter at home."

After they ate, they went out for a walk. The night was beautiful, and Julieta and Daniel wanted to show Sofia the new bars that hadn't been there on her first visit to the city, and some old ones she hadn't seen on that trip. That brought them to the Yasmine. Sofía tried to read the poster that apparently told the story of the Madame Yasmine the place was named after, but the lights were too low and she couldn't see well without her glasses. She asked Daniel, who tended to know the old stories of the Barrio Chino, but he couldn't remember. "But if they called her Madame, she must've been a whore," he declared. Then he asked them to wait a second, and returned in a bit with Manuel, a friend from the neighborhood. Daniel introduced him as one of the few cool Catalans he knew. Manuel had short dreadlocks and wore a black-and-white-striped shirt. Julieta explained that he worked with them in sound design on videos. "Our Argentine friend here wants to know the legends of the Barrio Chino," Daniel told him. Julieta asked him about Madame Yasmine, the bar's eponym.

"Let's see if I can be of service to the lady," Manuel said, smiling. He was a little drunk. He said that Yasmine's story was famous. She'd been born in the Barrio Chino at the end of the nineteenth century, the daughter of a flower vendor. And, of course, she was poor, and turned to prostitution. The Barrio Chino was a reeking hellhole then, and she was the madam in a brothel frequented by poets and anarchists. She fell in love with one of the anarchists and they had a child. But Franco's followers killed him—the anarchist— and she opened an opium den. Then the child was killed, decapitated by a cart on Las Ramblas, Manuel told them. He didn't have any more details about the death; the legend said only that a cart had cut off the boy's head, but nothing about how it happened.

"Oh, how awful," said Julieta. And Manuel went on to say

that Yasmine shut herself up in her house and set to smoking opium and emptying bottles. She went out once a week to do the shopping at La Boqueria, always carrying a headless doll in her arms. And, Manuel said, the doll's neck was made of her dead son's skin.

"What a lovely story to finish off the night," laughed Daniel, but he lit a cigarette a little nervously. The phrase had sounded stupid, uncomfortable.

"The building where she lived was around here, that's why they called this place Madame Yasmine. But they knocked it down when they built the Rambla del Raval."

"The depressing Rambla del Raval," said Daniel.

"*Tío*, there's a reason they call it Rambla Triste. They say the little boy is still wandering around here, without his head. One of Barcelona's many ghost children . . ."

"Manuel, please, you know I can't listen to that stuff," Julieta snapped.

And then Manuel smiled at Sofía and said, "Satisfied? I have more stories, but you'll have to have coffee with me sometime, because our little friend here can't handle horror stories." And then, without waiting for a reply, he asked Daniel about the dates of their next meetings to retouch a video they were working on, and the conversation turned toward names Sofía didn't know and work disagreements she wasn't interested in. Since the work talk also involved Julieta, Sofía could sit a while in silence, almost alone, thinking about the neck made of dead skin. Suddenly the bar, with its date salads and designer cocktails, struck her as horrible, and all she wanted was to get out of there. But she waited until her friends started to yawn.

. . .

The next night, Sofía and Julieta went out alone—they wanted a girls' night. Daniel was delighted to let them go, so he could stay home and catch up on all the unwatched episodes of his favorite shows. He would rather watch TV than go out in the Barcelona night, he said, and he seemed to mean it.

When Julieta closed the door to the building, she grabbed her friend by the arm, hard. "I don't want to go to La Concha and see drag queens," she said. The shows weren't what they used to be, anyway, Julieta told her; now they were full of bachelorette parties, and half the time the performers just went around greeting the brides-to-be. There were even little kids who went now. It was going downhill, it was sad. The queens used to be so splendid and ferocious, it was depressing to see them dressed as Marisa Paredes, putting on a show for all audiences. No and no. Julieta wanted to go to a bar. She wanted to talk. She wanted to tell Sofía things she never would have dared say in her emails or letters, or in their rare phone conversations. "I had a rough time of it last year," she said, and she started to cry in her particular way, suddenly and with big, heavy tears that she'd held back for a long time. Sofía pulled her into the first open bar she saw, and handed Julieta her tissues. The same smell floated around them, stagnant and constant, but Julieta didn't seem to notice. It wasn't the right moment to ask her friend if she smelled it too.

They ordered coffee. Neither of them wanted to drink alcohol. Julieta calmed down a bit, and then was able to talk. She'd gone crazy, she said. Maybe from thinking so much about all the crazy people in Barcelona.

"There's always some event going on in this city, some Bi-ennale, some presidential meeting, a Barça game. And then there are helicopters everywhere, flying low, you can't imagine how intense it is."

Sofía nodded; she could imagine.

"And last year Daniel and I wanted to . . . well, I wanted to get pregnant. I was really crazy, seriously. Now it seems like lunacy, wanting to raise a child, no money, what a disaster. And also . . . well, I'll get to that."

Julieta looked behind her, as if she felt a presence. She breathed in relief, and went on.

"The thing is that last year, I wanted to have a baby at any cost. But when we started to try I got the idea that the helicopters were coming after me. That they were flying around up there just to watch me."

"Oh, Julieta."

"I know, you don't have to say anything, I was paranoid. Just last month I stopped taking mood stabilizers. I miss them a little, but I have to get through it. So: I thought they were coming to get me, so they could take me and the baby to experiment on—some kind of science fiction delusion. Or else they wanted to steal the baby from me. They were, how can I explain it, like a kidnapping commando unit of the city of Barcelona. That's how serious it got. Daniel only realized it much later. He was working all day back then, I don't even remember on what, but it was an important video. I hid from the helicopters under the bed. Or I made tents with the sheets. I didn't want to go outside. One day Daniel found me there and, well, he took me to a shrink. The poor guy was really scared."

"Did you get pregnant?"

"No. Weird, because we went about six months without protection. Maybe one of us can't have kids. In any case, when I started treatment I had to stop trying, because the pills aren't recommended for pregnant women. Plus, I realized that wanting to have kids was part of my madness."

Julieta took the last sip of her coffee, and lowered her voice.

"No one should have kids in Barcelona. You heard what Manuel told us last night? This isn't a place for kids."

"What did he tell us?"

"You know! You think Yasmine's baby is the only kid wandering around Barcelona? Manuel told you."

Julieta's eyes were completely opaque, and her smile had frozen on her face with a rigidity that was the opposite extreme of happiness. Sofia thought her friend must still be crazy, that she'd have to have a talk with Daniel as soon as they got back to the apartment. Julieta took her hand on the table. Her fingers were cold, and she was trembling.

"You already know," she said.

"Know what, Juli, for the love of God."

"You've smelled it. The stench of the kids. I saw you wrinkling your nose."

Sofia shivered. Julieta told her she needed to tell her everything. She said that when she and Daniel came to Raval in 1997, the neighborhood was up in arms. The biggest pedophile ring in Europe had one of its main tentacles there, and people talked about children who were sold by their prostitute mothers to be photographed in bedrooms, kids whose poverty-stricken mothers left them in the hands of a pedophile named Xavier Tamarit. Children who were hunted down by pedophiles in Plaza Negra. They shut down an orphanage, and no one knew who the kids were; the priests and nuns had shredded their records. Kids who never went to school, who carried knives, who turned tricks. One of the boys stank; he stank because his one and only set of clothes was also his mattress. That kid wanders around the city, he fills it with his stench so no one ever forgets him. They say the social workers couldn't get the clothes off him because they were stuck to his body with dirt. They say he had lice, but also white worms in his scalp, and sores under his arms, from the dirt; no one had ever bathed him. He was a little animal, he shat himself from fear and didn't clean it off. That's the kid most people see, the most popular ghost, the one who touches you with his black hands, the one who brushes against the jacket slung over your chair and leaves it stinking of dead meat. But there are also kids who fell off balconies after their junkie mothers left them there. Kids who had keys hung around their necks at three, four years old. Kids who murdered taxi drivers and died of overdoses, whored themselves out, went looking for crack.

After the Tamarit case, the city started paying people forty thousand pesetas to leave their apartments. It was the most densely populated neighborhood in the world after Calcutta. Houses were falling down, there was no electricity, anyone with a bathroom was lucky, there was no running water.

Physically eradicate Barrio Chino. Operation: Illa Negra. Calles Nou, Sant Ramón, Marquès de Barberà.

On one wall someone painted the words "accumulando rabia"—Rage Accumulation.

The Raval prostitution case was an excuse to criminalize movement in the neighborhood, exploited by the instigators of the Old City's reform.

Tamarit is not aggressive, my exploration with the patient demonstrates he has the capacity of inhibition, he rationalizes his pedophilia but he has received chemical castration treatments to lower his libido, anatomical penis reduction, shrinkage, fibrosis, urethral stenosis, several operations.

The case had been an ambush, Julieta explained, a fraud. They used it to expel hordes of people, to clean up the neighborhood. Some belonged to one neighborhood party, others to another, she didn't understand it very well, but they were all problems of the Cataluñan Generalitat. A political matter.

But no one talked about the Raval case anymore. And why not? Julieta knew why. Because if it was ever discussed again, they would have to talk about the kids. Not about the raped children, because apparently there were no raped children, it was all a lie. About the other kids. The ones who were not alive.

"There's one who always walks down Tallers saying, 'I swear it on all my dead.' I thought he was real, at first, but no, because he always walks at the same time and not everyone sees him. Just awful, that's a lovely street, with all the record stores. . . . But sometimes I can't bring myself to go. Plus, he's out of his territory, that's the Gothic Quarter."

"Girl, you've got to—"

"Don't treat me like I'm *crazy*. Everyone in this city knows and they all act the idiot. But you already know, I can see it in your face. Which one did you see?"

Sofía looked down at her coffee, now cold. Then she raised

her eyes and looked over at the other tables. Two very tall Scandinavians were drinking beer beside them, speaking a strange language full of the letter "a." At the cigarette machine, two Catalans were sliding coins into the slot. On the walls, posters from shows at the Sidecar, exhibitions at the Museum of Contemporary Art. The English were cementing their bad reputation by shouting in the street, singing some possibly classic song that was unrecognizable in their drunken rendition. It all seemed normal, a city with exclusive locales—like that one that served only fresh fruit juices and smoothies—and designer clothing stores, tourists marveling at the modernist architecture, and girls enjoying the beach at Barceloneta. Sofía was afraid she was letting herself be influenced by her friend's paranoia, which seemed to confirm her own unease. What if her apprehension only came from a deep antipathy for proud Barcelona? What if hers was the phobia of a provincial tourist? She'd just decided to keep quiet when the smell inundated her nose like a hot pepper, like strong mint, making her eyes water; a smell that was almost palpable, black, from the crypt.

"I haven't seen anything," said Sofía. She was telling the truth. But she did believe Julieta. And she believed she would see before long.

Julieta seemed disappointed, frightened. But Sofía soothed her by squeezing her hand, and went on:

"But I smelled it. I smell it."

Sofía felt like gagging. She held it back by breathing deeply and using the napkin to block the smell a little.

"You smelled it where?" murmured Julieta.

"Everywhere. Right now."

"You know what they do? They don't let you leave."

"What?"

"The kids won't let people leave. We can't leave Raval. The kids were unhappy, they don't want anyone to go, they want to make people suffer. They suck you in. When you try to leave, they make you lose your passport. Or miss your plane. Or the taxi crashes on the way to the airport. Or you get a job offer you can't refuse because it's a lot of money. They're like the spirits in those stories, the ones that move things around in the house at night, but much worse. Anyone who says they don't want to leave Raval is lying. They *can't* leave. And they learn to live with it."

Sofía closed her eyes. She thought she could hear the quick footsteps of children running barefoot through the refurbished apartments of Raval, and she pictured a boy who used his filthy clothes as a mattress, so angry, so unhappy. She could almost see his toothless mouth, his old misery. She didn't want to see him for real, sitting in one of the doorways on Escudellers, using a junkie's old blanket. She didn't want to see the nocturnal rounds he made with his friends in Plaza Negra.

"You're leaving tomorrow," Julieta told her, serious now, and protective. "We'll change your ticket. I'll help you. You're just visiting. They can't trap visitors."

And then, following the lights of a helicopter that was crossing the sky northward, she murmured:

"Go home. Leave us here. And don't worry. We'll get out someday. Someday soon."

The Lookout

The Lady Upstairs always wanted to tell the girl, the daughter of the current owner, not to be afraid. There was nothing to fear. She was there, it was true, but the girl couldn't sense her, didn't see her; no one could sense her, unless, of course, she took on shape. But without shape she was denied presence. It wasn't that the girl had any special sensitivity: she was just terrified. She went running past the stairs that led to the hotel's lookout, imagining that there, in the tower—which for years had been the tallest building in Ostende—a crazy woman was hiding, a witch with long hair who wore a white nightgown and gazed at herself in a mirror. The girl was afraid, too, of the Italian cook who added wood to the boiler, afraid of him even after he was fired (she thought she might still come upon him in the hallways, lying in wait, and that he'd throw her on the fire along with the wood). Now that she was a grown woman, the owner's daughter didn't spend winters in the hotel. She said she couldn't stand the mediocrity of the solitary resort in the freezing winters, nothing but wind, not even a movie theater open in Pinamar; she said she was also afraid the place would be robbed. But those were lies. She still felt the same fear that had paralyzed her in the hotel's circular hallways when she was little; it was the same fear that kept her away from the practically monastic dining room on the first floor, or from the big mirror awaiting restoration in the guest room used for storage, where she was afraid of seeing something unknown reflected.

Strange. And even odder was what people said—the guests, the owner himself. There was the story of the worker who died during construction and was bricked up in the wall, as if the hotel aspired to be a Gothic cathedral. Then there was the guest who claimed to hear sounds of a party coming from the main dining room, which dissolved with a cautious hiss when she tried to approach. A cook confirmed the rumors of the celebrating ghosts. All false. The Lady Upstairs was the one tasked with finding for the hotel the thing that all those people feared or invented. And she had never managed it. Not when the Belgians abandoned the hotel to go to war. Not during the years of sand, when the building was buried up to the second floor. Not even during the summer of the whale, with all those flies that invaded the beach with their death buzz, feeding on the lifeless animal run aground. The summer no one went swimming.

Yes, desperate people stayed at the hotel. Yes, she'd heard them mutter death wishes and she'd bestowed on them dreams of terrible childhoods and forgotten pain. But none had been ready. And it was a lie that time didn't pass for beings like her. She was tired. She longed for each summer to be the last, and she spent more and more time in the lookout tower, where she could barely hear the whisper of the living, which she knew how to imitate so well, but could not comprehend.

And if this damned jacket won't fit in the suitcase, I'm going to freeze to death, it's cold at night on the coast, thought Elina, and she couldn't help it, she started crying again like she always did these days with every little setback. Like when the dining room lamp burned out and she didn't have a replacement bulb, or any idea how to change it; like when she forgot to pay the electricity bill and had to cross the city to the company's offices; like when she ran out of pills and went searching for an all-night pharmacy at four in the morning. She had taken leave from the university, and she'd tried to fake a certain amount of sanity with family and friends, but it was so difficult that she no longer answered the phone and barely replied to emails and they would just have to deal with it; she didn't care how worried they were. She didn't even inform them that she'd stopped going to therapy and was just taking the pills; she had nothing more to talk about or dig up, she just wanted that vaguely distant, chemically induced state that disconnected her but still let her live a little. Less and less, but enough.

She didn't even really want to go to the hotel, but she'd promised herself she would months ago, before the hospital, back when she still thought that a week at the ocean could make her feel better, force her to stop thinking about Pablo. He had left and he hadn't called her again, or written; she didn't know if he was alive or dead and she would prefer either possibility, either of them, to this suspended life of waiting for him for a year now. As always, she sent him a message to let him know where she would be. She even included the phone number. She was going to spend her birthday at the hotel. If Pablo was alive, if he had ever loved her, he had to call.

She missed his caresses on her back, missed his laughing at her paranoia, his useless attempts to console her, the hours it took him to bathe, how he practically didn't like to eat, the bones of his hips, his way of moving his hands when he talked; she wanted to look at his photos again and get jealous when he paid more attention to the cat than to her and to walk in the sun beside him in his ever-present sunglasses; she missed the early morning phone calls and watching him sleep and how he knew to stay quiet and how she got irritated when he stayed quiet too long and the mornings begging him not to leave and crying when he left even if he'd be back in two hours and she never, ever would have left him like that, no news, no goodbye, ungrateful, but what if he was dead because it was possible he was, no one had ever heard from him again unless they were hiding it from her, but how could they hide something like that when they'd seen her vomit blood from not eating, when they'd seen her biting her pillow until she tore the case, when they'd seen her hurting herself and drunk and waiting hours for an email with her eyes fixed on the screen until she had a headache and blood-shot eyes and was crying onto the keyboard, never going out and waiting for a phone call; they'd heard her say to hell with all that bullshit about out with the old and in with the new life goes on you have to get laid there are thousands of men out there you look great let's go dancing I want to introduce you to someone.

The Lady Upstairs liked this new girl, but over the years she'd learned not to trust first impressions. She remembered that time, almost twenty years before, when she'd seen a blond woman arrive, her nose red from crying and her eyes dull and staring; that same night she learned that the woman was spending some days at the hotel in order to be close to the sea and try to console herself, a little, over the death of her son. The Lady Upstairs had taken the form of a small child and appeared to the woman in the hallways, in the room, near the beach, on the stairs that led to the first floor, but the woman only screamed and screamed and they took her away in the ambulance. She was with her husband. That had been a lesson: only try with women who are alone.

The new girl's name was Elina, and she was alone. She was beautiful, but she didn't know it. She had the sunken eyes of insomnia and too many cigarettes; she wore a defiant expression and she was gruff with the charming and loqua-cious owners. She didn't even look at the other guests. The first day, she didn't go down to the beach, or to breakfast, or to lunch, and at dinner she pushed the food around on her plate and surreptitiously took three pills with her wine. She could tell Elina hated the beach. Then why was she there? Something had happened to her on a beach, years before. She'd have to find out that night, so Elina would remember it in her dreams.

The Lady moved down the blue carpeted hallways to Elina's room. The girl had paid for one of the better ones, a suite with a microwave and refrigerator, but she clearly wasn't going to use any of the amenities. It still wasn't the right moment to take shape. Tomorrow. Tonight it was enough for Elina to dream of that night on the beach, when she was seventeen years old and thought she was indestructible; that night when she'd left the bar and agreed to go with the drunk man to the empty beach. He had covered her mouth to keep her from screaming, but Elina hadn't even moved, frozen from fear. And afterward she hadn't told anyone. She had just showered, and she'd cried, and she'd bought some intimate creams to allay the smell and the stinging from the sand that burned her soft internal skin.

What a perfect time to remember that shit, thought Elina, and she looked out the window of her room, which had a view of the pool. It's not that she'd forgotten, but it was rare for that night on the beach to appear in her dreams. But she knew that it was why Pablo had left her. Because sometimes he touched her and she remembered the sand between her legs and the pain, and she had to say *enough*, and she'd never been able to explain anything because of the fear, until he'd gotten fed up, and why wouldn't he, when she was ruined forever.

Outside, she saw a couple talking, each on a lounge chair, holding hands. She hated them. The kids were in the pool even though it wasn't hot, and a man some fifty years old was reading a book with a yellow cover in the shade. Only a few guests, or at least that was the feeling the hotel gave, silent as it was. This was not a good idea, thought Elina, and she waited an hour, two hours, but no one rang from reception to let her know she had a call. Thirty-one years of so much not knowing what to do. What to do. Twenty more years teaching classes at the university. Twenty more years as an *adjunct*. Twenty years of not enough money and then dying alone; twenty years of faculty meetings and complaints. She had no other plan. And moreover, if she had to be frank, it was possible she couldn't even be an *adjunct* anymore. In her last class, she'd started to cry while explaining Durkheim—what a moron. She'd run out of the room. She couldn't forget the way the kids giggled, more out of nervousness than cruelty, but how she would have liked to murder them. She'd locked herself in the teachers' lounge and someone found her there, trembling. Someone else called an ambulance, and she didn't remember much more until she woke up in a clinic— expensive, with charming and unbearable professionals, paid for by her mother. And then the group therapy sessions, and the horrible feeling that she didn't care about what the others said, and thinking about how to die while she participated in arts-and-crafts activities ("Could I stab myself in the jugular with this paintbrush?"), and the individual therapy sessions when she kept quiet because she couldn't explain anything, and then her dubious discharge. Her parents had rented an apartment for her so she could be independent, so she could recover more quickly, so she could integrate—all those commonplaces. And Pablo, who hadn't even asked about her, wherever he was. And going back to the university for a month at the psychiatrist's insistence, though she had managed only two weeks, and then sick leave, and now the beach.

She pulled her hair back in a sloppy ponytail and decided to have lunch—as usual she had woken up late, because she no longer monitored the number of pills she was taking. And then, she told herself, to the beach. The sun was out. Supposedly the ocean was calming. When she went out, she passed some strange sculptures of sheep that seemed straight out of a giant nativity scene, and she looked with something like curiosity at two teenagers playing at tossing a cork into the mouth of a bronze frog.

Again, she pushed the food around on her plate, but she managed to get two mouthfuls down, and an entire 7UP—at least it was sugar. And she headed off to the beach, which was only a block away. The access was a pebbled path lined by shrubs that cut her breath short—what if something was hiding there—but she ran along it and reached the old wooden steps and then the sea. It was an enormous beach, with sand that was lighter and more diaphanous than the rest of the coast, and a violet-blue sky that now looked like rain. She sat down in one of the chairs under an awning and looked at some men, forty-something but still slender, who were playing soccer. She thought about approaching them, maybe taking one of them to bed—why not? she hadn't had sex in a year—but she knew it wouldn't happen, people can smell desperation, and she reeked. She saw girls defying the wind in their bikinis, and she waited for the rain to come, she let it soak her. And when her long hair was dripping onto her pants, when the cold water was running from her neck to her chest and belly, she took the razor out of her pocket and started making precise cuts on her arm, one, two, three, until she saw the blood and felt the pain and something similar to an orgasm. Let it stay cold, so she could cover herself. Though she didn't really care. She was only afraid some charitable soul would notice, take pity on her, and make the feared phone call to Buenos Aires or the ambulance or the suicide hotline.

When she returned to the hotel she asked if she had received any calls. "No, dear," the receptionist told her, all smiles. In the room, she sank into the bathtub and went back over the cuts, so the blood would float around her and turn the water red. It was beautiful. She put her head underwater and opened her eyes to an ocean of reddish swirls.

She didn't want to talk to anyone, but at breakfast there was a girl who'd just arrived—Elina assumed, because she was very pale and seemed uncomfortable—who sat down at her table. In the morning the dining room filled up. Elina ordered coffee with milk to stay awake, because she hadn't slept at all and was feeling dizzy. Her heart pounded in her chest with the first rush of caffeine, but she didn't care. How lovely to die like that, suddenly and without planning, in such a simple way. Much better than pills: when she'd tried that, when she'd woken up with a tube down her throat, she'd realized how hard it was to manage an overdose. Later, she realized her mistake, she learned which pills she should have taken, but didn't dare try again.

After a shy hello, the girl asked her if she'd gone up to Saint-Exupéry's room. Elina told her not yet, though she was thinking, *What the hell do I care about some writer's room.* The girl insisted, though not out of any literary zeal. "I heard that if you take photos in there, they always come out blurry. They say his ghost appears in the image. I don't know, but this hotel sure deserves a ghost."

"Maybe," Elina told her, "but Saint-Exupéry's doesn't scare me, to be honest." The girl laughed. She had a strange laugh, forced but not fake, as if she weren't used to laughing. Elina liked her. Or at least she didn't find her as distasteful as the rich, waxed kids, or the gentlemen of such interesting conversation, the carefree girls with their bespectacled boyfriends carrying books under their arms, or the forty-somethings who in the evenings uncorked expensive wines and sniffed them, sighing before lighting up a cigar.

"And do you know about the lookout tower?" asked the girl.

"A little," said Elina. "Just that they don't show it to everyone, because the structure is old, they didn't renovate it and it's dangerous." The girl shook her head. She had long hands, but she was very short. The effect was disproportionate—she almost looked deformed. "It's not dangerous. The stairs are steep. I've seen it. We could go. They don't lock it, that's a lie. The door sticks a little. You just have to push it."

"Okay," said Elina. "Let's go tomorrow." She asked for that twenty-four-hour grace period to give herself a chance to sleep. And, more importantly, to find an internet café in case Pablo had written.

But she never made it to the café. She recognized the shaking in her hands, the shortness of breath, the need to get out of her body, that thinking always of the same thing. She lit a cigarette in the hallway and went back to the room smoking, to wait for the night and the next day lying faceup on the bed, the TV on though she couldn't understand the meaning of any of the programs, terrified because she couldn't cry.

Beings like The Lady Upstairs didn't get excited or worked up. They were just sure. And she was sure that Elina was the one. That she was going to do it.

She'd brought her to the lookout tower. It was true that the owners locked the door leading to the wooden staircase, so steep; but of course those tools couldn't stop her. Elina had followed her up, panting a little. She had gotten a splinter in her hand on the way up, but she didn't even cry out. And when they reached the square space of the lookout—the windows from where, when you stood on tiptoe and breathed in the scent of the wood, you could see the ocean in the distance, the sepia light and the shadows below, in a kind of hollow beneath the tower—she saw Elina smile.

"The owner's daughter, when she was little, thought the crazy lady was hiding up here."

"What crazy lady?" Elina was still smiling.

"None, there never was one. She'd read some book with a

crazy woman locked in a tower and she started to believe it was real."

"They always lock up the crazy ladies in books," murmured Elina.

"They could escape."

"They could," said Elina, and she sat down on the floor to toy with shards of glass left over from a renovation that was never finished. "I had a birthday yesterday," she said. "Thirty-one years old."

"And you didn't want to celebrate?"

Elina looked at her, and the girl smiled, although surely that was not the thing to do. Maybe she should hug Elina, as she sometimes saw people do. But that could ruin everything.

Better to bring her to the tower again, the next day.

And lock her in.

And maybe reveal her true form before leaving her alone up there.

And keep the guests and the owners from hearing her screams. The Lady Upstairs was capable of controlling what reached people's ears and what didn't.

And wait for her to grow desperate from hunger, and talk to her from the other side of the door, tell her how no one would come looking for her, because no one cared about her.

Maybe even go in again, several times if necessary, and each time show something more of her true form. And her true smell. And, of course, her true touch. Oh, she knew that nothing was as terrifying as her touch.

And wait for the impact, the sound, the screams: Elina had looked closely not only at the windows, but also at the stairs. One wrong step on those stairs would be enough. And if not, she could climb them again, and throw herself down again from the top. She was capable of doing that.

And then the hotel would have Elina to wander in circles with her cold hands and her bloody arms.

And The Lady Upstairs would be free, because at last she'd found the one.

Where Are You, Dear Heart?

I have three memories of him, but one of them could be false. The order is arbitrary. In the first he is sitting on a sofa, completely naked, on a towel, watching TV. He doesn't pay any attention to me: I think I'm spying on him. His penis rests in a tangle of black hair, and the scar that cuts through his chest hair is dark pink.

In the second, his wife is leading him by the hand to the bedroom. He's naked again. He looks at me sideways. His hair is pretty long, even for the time—the seventies—and I can't see his scar.

In the third he smiles at me from up close, his face almost touching mine. In the memory I feel naked and shy. But I don't know if it's real; it doesn't have the same naturalness as the others and I might have made it up, though I recognize that feeling of shyness and vulnerability that often repeats in my dreams. I don't know if he touched me. The sensation that accompanies his memory is something like desire, when, if my suspicions are true, it should be more like horror. I'm not afraid of him, his face doesn't torment me, even though I've tried to dredge up something like childhood trauma and its consequences in my adult life. I was five years old when I met him. He was very sick—he'd had a heart operation and it had gone badly. I found that out later, after I stopped going to his house—really, the house of his daughters, my friends. I found it out when he died. I don't remember what his name was, and I've never dared to ask my parents.

Sometime after his death, I started using my nails to mark my chest right in the center, imitating his scar. I did it before falling asleep, naked, and I'd raise my head to look at the line of irritated skin until it disappeared and my neck started to ache.

When it was very hot, I liked to go into the spare bedroom; it was the coolest in the house, the only room no one went into, because Mom used it for storing old books and furniture. I adored that room: I liked to stretch out naked on the leather sofa, always cold, bring in a little fan and read all afternoon. My friends from the neighborhood and from school were all at the club pool, but I didn't care: in that room I'd fallen hopelessly in love, for the first time, when I discovered Helen Burns in a battered edition of *Jane Eyre*, illustrated.

I hated those illustrations. Because they depicted Helen as much bigger than the book described her, and because for some reason they'd depicted her as blond, though the book never mentioned her hair color. She didn't look like that, and I would know, because I spent that whole summer picturing her on the sofa that had become the orphanage bed, the very bed where Helen—consumptive, moribund, and so beautiful—died while I held her hand.

Helen was a minor character in the book. Jane, the protagonist, arrived at the dreadful school for young girls called Lowood, and she couldn't make friends with anyone because the evil director Brocklehurst had humiliated her in front of all her classmates. But Helen didn't care: Helen became Jane's friend. She was beyond all that, because she was near death. I sensed I was going to fall in love with her when Jane saw her for the first time on the veranda, reading that book with such a strange name, *Rasselas*. One more chapter and Helen was dead. Typhus broke out at the school, Helen suffered a relapse of her tuberculosis and was moved to an upstairs room, and Jane snuck in to visit her one night. That final night, Helen and Jane slept together. Today, when I remember that chapter (because I don't need to reread it, I know it by heart), I understand everything: when Jane gets into the dying girl's bed and Helen says to her, "Are you warm, darling?" Darling. Darling. It was a love scene. When Jane woke up, her friend Helen was dead. That chapter: every night, every one, I lay down and hugged my pillow and pretended it was Helen, but I didn't fall asleep like that idiot Jane, oh no. I watched her die, I held her hand, and she, who was expiring with her gray gaze fixed on my eyes as she fought for breath, allowed me to see something of that other place where she would spend eternity.

I soon realized that my fantasy was unattainable. When I was fourteen, a friend said to me, remorsefully:

"Guess what I heard. You remember Mara's brother?"

Mara was an ex-classmate who had moved to another school.

"Yeah."

"Well, they found out he has a tumor between his heart and lungs, and they can't operate on it, so he's going to die."

One week later I was suggesting to my friend that we visit Mara. I wanted to meet her dying brother, because I suspected that, well, that I could fall in love with him. But when I met him . . . the boy seemed sick enough, but I didn't find him attractive. It was a confusing time for me, and I reached a conclusion that soothed my conscience: I didn't like real sick people, and as such, I was not depraved. Those thoughts didn't save me from my obsession. For an entire year I spent my allowance on expensive medical books, while my friends all spent theirs on drugs. Nothing brought me as much happiness as those books. All those euphemisms for death. All those beautiful medical terms that didn't mean anything, all that hard jargon—*that* was pornography. By then I was pretty clear on what turned me on and what didn't, and so I was increasingly bored by Victorian novels, where there was always some sick person but you never really knew what they were dying of. I was a little fed up with all the tuberculosis, once I'd gotten over my savage crush on Ippolit, the teenager with tuberculosis in *The Idiot*, which lasted over a year. I wanted pornography: sick people like Helen, Tadzio, or Ippolit were eroticism, suggestion. And they were always secondary characters. Ippolit was ideal: beautiful (Dostoyevsky made sure to have Prince Myshkin describe his "lovely face," a line that always made me tremble), adolescent, definitively dying and stubborn and vulnerable and wicked. But he talked a lot and fainted little: I was tired of reading descriptions of paleness and sweating and coughing. I wanted details, I wanted explicit sex.

The medical books were ideal, and they also helped me specify my fetishes. I skipped right over neurological illnesses: I didn't like convulsions or mental retardation or paralysis, and the nervous system definitely bored me. I could care less, oddly, about oncology: cancer seemed dirty, socially overvalued, a little vulgar ("the poor woman has a *tumor*," the old ladies would say), and there were too many movies about heroic cancer patients (I liked heroic patients, but not the ones who were *role models*). And how graceless was nephrology: clearly people died if their kidneys stopped working, but I didn't care, because just the word "kidney" struck me as awful. Not to mention gastrointestinal illnesses, so filthy.

It was clear what I liked, where I fell on the map, and once I'd clarified the specialty, I dedicated myself to it alone: I liked pulmonary illnesses (certainly reminiscent of Helen, Ippolit, and all the other tubercular patients), and cardiac patients. These latter had their tawdry side, but only if they were elderly (or over fifty, when frightful things like cholesterol started to intervene). If they were young . . . what elegance. Because, in general, you couldn't tell. If they were beautiful, it was a kind of secretly ruined beauty. All the other illnesses tended to have a timeline, but this one was different. A person could die at any moment. Once, I bought a CD in a medical bookstore (where all the employees thought I was a student—I'd been sure to slip that in, as a precaution) that was called *Cardiac Sounds*. Nothing had ever brought me so much joy. I guess that what normal men and women feel when they hear their preferred gender moaning in pleasure, I felt when I heard those ruined hearts beat. Such variety! So many different rhythms, all meaning something different, all of them beautiful! Other illnesses couldn't be *heard*. Plus, many of them could be *smelled*, which I found unpleasant. If I took my MP3 player out on a bike ride, I'd have to stop because I was too turned on. So I listened to it at night, at home, and during that time I got worried because *I wasn't interested in real sex*. The audio tracks of heartbeats took the place of everything. I could masturbate with my headphones on for hours, dripping wet between my legs, my arm cramping up from so much rubbing and my clitoris inflamed to the size of a giant grape.

After a while, I decided to get rid of the recorded heartbeats. They were going to drive me crazy. From then on, one of the first things I did with a man was lay my head on his chest, to see if there was any arrhythmia, or a murmur, an irregular beat, a third heart sound, or an atrial flutter, or anything else. I always wondered when I would find someone who was an unbeatable combination of elements. I remember that longing now, and I smile bitterly.

. . .

I can specify the exact moment I lost control. After years of sterile searching, I found a website where other heartbeat fetishists shared their hearts. They did it live, in chats, but they also had an extensive archive of sounds that you could download, deliciously classified into normal and abnormal beats, hearts during exercise, heart murmurs, ectopic heartbeats. . . . I never participated in the chats. I only copied those sounds and lay down to listen to them. An accelerated, regular rhythm; suddenly an early beat, another one delayed (premature atrial or ventricular contractions). And I thought my earlier masturbations had been brutal! I'd had no idea, I knew nothing about the limits of lust. My middle finger between my inner right labia and clitoris, rubbing until I hit bone, until my bone hurt, sometimes until I bled, and the orgasms came one after another, implacable, tremendous, for hours. The sheets damp, perspiration dripping down between my breasts, my skin always prickling, and the feeling of my swollen, glorious clitoris, and the contractions of my vagina and uterus. Supraventricular tachycardia, the beautiful sound of aortic stenosis, the irregular beats provoked by hyperventilation or the Valsalva maneuver, things only the brave would attempt. Sometimes a hidden heart, beating barely audibly and frenzied behind the ribs, a sound achieved by holding the breath; and when finally the oxygen returned, that heart shook itself as if it lived inside a can of tomatoes, disconcerted, sometimes too slow, as if it were about to stop.

I didn't answer the phone. I was late everywhere I went. I

only stopped when the pain of my irritated, sometimes wounded vulva took my pleasure away. In the dark with my headphones and the hearts, that was my life, and I'd never have sex with people again. What for?

Until I isolated one of the hearts. Its beat never, ever failed. I could distinguish it perfectly even without checking its author, who went by the name HCM1. The recordings were always very clear, and the beats always different, and dangerous: in atrial fibrillation, in long tachycardias, in a ventricular gallop. It was a man. I could hear him breathing sometimes, and there were vestiges of his voice. I found one sound file where he moaned because—said the text that accompanied the file—he'd felt pain in his chest during the session, and that was when I decided to enter the chat to meet him.

He was evasive for a while. Too long, it seemed to me, but I guess it was objectively a short time. A month after our first contact, he agreed to visit me. Strange: we lived in the same city. Statistically unlikely, if not impossible, because we had met in an international fetish community. We decided not to ascribe any importance to the coincidence, not to fall into ideas about messages from fate or theories like that. We just dove into pleasure. He liked to have his heart listened to. He was very sick, and so he tended to get rejected in chats and online communities. People thought he was too extreme, that he went too far, that he ruined the idea of play and pleasure. Soon we both abandoned the online life, and we locked ourselves in my room with a sound recorder, a stethoscope, medicines and substances that helped change his cardiac rhythm. We both knew how it could end, and we didn't care.

. . .

His hair was as dark as that of the man I'd met as a child, and his smile was the same. But he had three scars, not just one. They'd opened his sternum from top to bottom: a casual observer would have seen a single scar, but I could tell them apart. The first one transparent, thin, almost totally hidden by the second, of an opaline pink that shone like it was coated in polish; the last one, broader, brutal, was darker than his skin. The scar that crossed his back (he'd described that painful process in detail) was enormous, clumsy. The small, discreet scars on his stomach seemed to be distributed randomly. The skin on the inside of his arm was marked like a drug addict's. There was another short scar, a dark sinking on the right side of his neck. So many marks. And his labored breathing, and his fleshy lips that sometimes took on a color as blue as his eyes.

I could hear his illness. It was in those sudden inhalations when he ran out of breath as he spoke, in the nocturnal coughing attacks that left him pale and trembling. He always let me rest my head on his chest, to listen. A normal beat is two sounds, open and close. But his beats had four sounds, a gallop, a desperate effort, different and unnatural. It got worse with a cup of coffee. It was scary with a little cocaine. He fainted often, and I went on listening through the stethoscope, terrified and excited, until his heartbeat recovered a kind of normalcy and he woke up. I could spend hours on his chest and then, thrilled, I kissed and embraced him almost violently, and his laughter and abandon worried me, because at times—ever more often as our intimacy grew—I was certain that if I listened one second longer, I was going to wound him even more. Hitting him, clawing him with my nails, scarring him more, was a way of being even closer, of making him more mine. I had to contain that desire, that wish to sate myself, to open him up, play with his organs like hidden trophies. It got to the point that I imposed little punishments on myself: not eating all day, going seventy-two hours without sleeping, walking until my legs cramped up. . . . Little rituals, the same way a girl wishes death on her mother because she won't buy her something, and then feels remorse and makes little sacrifices: "I won't say any more bad words, God, I promise, but don't let my mom die." And the bad word slips out and then comes the running in at night to be sure the mother is still breathing in bed while she sleeps.

But I think I ended up hating him. Maybe I hated him from the start. Just like I hated the man who had made me abnormal, who'd made me sick, with his tired penis in front of the TV, and that beautiful scar. The man who'd ruined me. I hated my lover. Otherwise some of our games were inexplicable. I made him breathe quickly into a plastic bag until I saw his forehead grow damp and his arms start to tremble. His heart pounded in the stethoscope and he would beg, "Enough," but I asked for more, and he never said no. I had to take him to the hospital once, and while they regulated his tachycardia with cardioversion—an electrical discharge in the chest, like in resuscitations—I locked myself in a nearby bathroom and fell onto the toilet when I reached orgasm, howling. I bought him poppers, cocaine, tranquilizers, alcohol. Each substance caused a different effect and he went along with all of it, he never complained, he hardly spoke. He even paid my rent with his savings when they threatened to kick me out of the apartment; I never paid again. I no longer had a phone, I only worried about the electricity for the sound recorder, so I could go back and listen to my experiments when he was too exhausted, nearly unconscious.

He didn't even protest when I told him I was bored. That I wanted to see it. Rest my hand on his heart stripped of ribs, of cages, have it in my hand beating until it stopped, feel the desperate valves open and shut in the fresh air. He only said that he was tired too.

And that we were going to need a saw.

Meat

So some of him lived but the most of him died.

RUDYARD KIPLING, "THE VAMPIRE"

All the TV shows, newspapers, magazines, and radio programs wanted to talk to the girls: Julieta, the younger, and Mariela, the older. The television vans stayed parked outside the psychiatric clinic where they were hospitalized for over a week, but the reporters got nothing. When the girls were released, the cameramen took off after them, some getting tangled in the cables, a few falling onto the concrete. But the girls weren't running away. They looked into the cameras with smiles that were later described as "terrifying" and "cryptic," and they got into the car that Mariela's father drove away. The girls' parents wouldn't talk either: the cameras could only record their nervous pacing through the hospital hallways, their fearful eyes, and Julieta's mother sobbing when she came out of her house with a bag full of clothes.

The silence provoked an extreme hysteria. The front pages of the newspapers talked about the most shocking case of teenage fanaticism not only in Argentina, but in the whole world. The story was picked up by international media outlets. Psychiatrists and psychologists were called in as experts; the case monopolized the news, the gossip shows, the afternoon tabloid and talk shows, and the radio talked of nothing else. Julieta and Mariela, sixteen and seventeen years old, two girls from Mataderos who were fans of Santiago Espina, the rock star who in less than a year had left the suburbs behind to fill theaters and stadiums in downtown Buenos Aires; Santiago, whom the music press loved and hated in equal measure: he was a genius, he was pretentious, he was an unclassifiable artist, he was a commercial artifact for hypnotizing alienated girls, he was the future of Argentine music, he was a capricious idiot. El Espina—as he was known by both his worshippers and his detractors—had stupefied the critics with his second album, *Meat*, eleven songs that split opinions even further: on one side they called it a masterpiece; on the other, a self-indulgent anachronism. Sales skyrocketed, and the record label started to dream about an international release. Santiago Espina was strange, yes, he was unpredictable and almost never gave interviews, but how could he refuse promotional tours through Mexico, Chile, Spain? They just had to convince him to finally make a video once and for all, so the world could get a glimpse of his eyes and the way his pants hugged the sharp bones of his hips.

One month after *Meat* sold out, the city—papered end to

end with Espina's face—received the news that he had disappeared, mere days before he was going to present his hit album at Obras Stadium. Tickets were sold out. His fans—almost all of them girls, which only increased his detractors' contempt—sobbed in spontaneous gatherings in the street, organized marches, and recited *Meat* lyrics in an ecstatic litany, kneeling before posters of Espina Scotch-taped to monuments and trees in all the plazas of Buenos Aires, as if praying to a moribund god.

As the desperation was spreading to teenagers in the country's interior, the discovery of Espina's body provoked an unheard-of terror among disoriented parents. Santiago's body had been found in a hotel room near the Once Station, his whole body flayed: he had used a razor and a knife to carefully skin his arms, legs, stomach. On his left arm, he'd sliced to the bone. In his chest you could see his sternum. And finally, possibly semi-unconscious, he'd slit his jugular with a bold, precise cut. He had not mutilated his face. One of the policemen charged with forcing the lock on the door of the room said that it had reminded him of a walk-in freezer: it was the middle of winter, and Santiago had left the air conditioner on. There were several conspiracy theories about a possible murder, but they were ruled out when it was leaked that the room had been locked with a key from the inside, and the suicide note was published, almost illegible because of the nervous handwriting and the bloodstains. It said: "Meat is food. Meat is death. You all know what the future holds." Ravings of a dying man, said the experts, and the fans were silent and cried locked in their rooms, where the teddy bears and pink-covered diaries mixed with always overloaded backpacks and photos of Espina, more beautiful than ever now that death shone in his eyes.

The nation expected an epidemic of teenage suicides that never came. The girls went back to school and to the clubs, and only one case of serious depression was recorded, in Mendoza. Still, the fans all listened to *Meat* as their idol's last will and testament, trying to decipher the album's lyrics in online forums and on long phone conversations. The press said goodbye to Santiago Espina with features and elegies, and for a time talked about nothing but suicide, drugs, and rock and roll. The funeral in Chacarita was less well attended and much sadder than expected, and the mourning subsided once the people close to the star finished their procession through TV programs. Santiago Espina was relegated to "important anniversaries," ready to be unearthed a year after his death, or on his birthday.

No one could have suspected that something was being hatched between two girls in Mataderos over a wrinkled photo of the suicide note, *Meat* on the stereo, start to finish, over and over.

Mariela had been one of the very first "Espinosas" (as the press called Santiago's fans, the girls with their eyes lined in mortuary black, cheap feather boas around their necks, and leopard-print pants). She had followed him for a year, night after night, wherever Espina played. She knew the suburban trains and buses well, and she'd spent freezing dawns

trembling on train platforms, the song list in her pocket, ca-
ressing the paper with her eyes closed. Espina knew her and
sometimes—very rarely, because he almost never spoke to
his audience, not even to announce songs or say good night—
he'd give her some small offering: his guitar pick or a plastic cup with a little beer in it. In the bathroom of a club in
Burzaco, she met Julieta, who was the most famous Espinosa
because she had tattooed the idol's name on her neck; from
far away, the letters looked like a scar, as if her head had been
sewn onto her neck. Julieta had managed to take a photo with
Espina: they both looked very serious, they weren't touching,
and the flash had turned their eyes red. Julieta and Mariela
lived just ten blocks apart, and Espina's suicide united them
so much that they started to resemble each other physically,
like couples who live together for decades or solitary people
who start to look like their pets.

That mimetic resemblance had surprised the cemetery
caretaker who'd found them in the early morning as they
were trying to jump the wall. "It was still dark," he said,
"but I never thought they were thieves. I could tell from far
away they were young girls, and when I got closer I saw they
were also twins." Julieta and Mariela didn't put up a fight
when the caretaker caught them. They seemed dazed, and
they let him lead them to the office; the man thought they
were on drugs, and he figured they'd spent the night in the
cemetery keeping vigil at Espina's grave. The caretaker and
his coworkers had found girls there before, hiding in the pas-
sageways of niches or behind trees around closing time, but
none of them had ever managed to stay with their idol until
dawn. The caretaker thought Julieta and Mariela had been

lucky, but as he was scolding them and asking for their parents' phone numbers, he noticed that the girls were covered in dirt, blood, and a film of muck that stank and was smeared all over their hands and clothes and faces. Then he called the police.

That afternoon the news filtered to the media. Two teenagers had dug up Santiago Espina's coffin using a shovel and their own hands. The grave, only a month after his burial, still didn't have the definitive marble slab that would have made their task more difficult. But the exhumation was just the beginning. The girls had opened the casket to feed on Espina's remains with devotion and disgust; around the grave, pools of vomit bore witness to their efforts. One of the policemen threw up too. "They left his bones clean," he told the TV reporter, who, shaken, was speechless for the first time in his career. The girls were brought in a patrol car to the station, and there it was decided they'd be taken to a private clinic. The police said that Julieta and Mariela had never cried, or even spoken to them; they only whispered into each other's ears and held hands the whole time. It was leaked that when the nurses at the clinic tried to bathe the girls, they resisted with such fury that one nurse ended up scratched and bitten; the girls were finally sedated and bathed in their sleep.

Talking to them, to their families, their doctors, became a priority. But they were all silent. Espina's family had decided not to press charges against Julieta and Mariela, in order "to put an end to this horror." The star's mother, it was said, went through life overloaded on tranquilizers. Stories of a previous suicide attempt by Espina couldn't be confirmed; nor could any girlfriend be found, only lovers who hadn't spent more than one night with him, and they had little to tell. The musicians in the band refused to talk to the press, but those who knew them said they were in shock, and, above all, disgusted. They all quit music for good. They had never had a great relationship with Santiago, they were his employees, or more like slaves who accepted his whims with resignation, out of ambition and a distant admiration.

Fans sat sullenly at televised round tables and panels to fight with hosts and psychologists. They had decided to avoid black clothes, and they appeared sprawled in armchairs with red lips, leopard pants, shiny shirts, and nails painted red, blue, green, pink. They answered questions with monosyllables, or sometimes ironic giggles. One of them, however, cried openly when she was asked what she thought about the girls who had eaten her idol. Defiantly, she shouted, "I envy them! They understood!" And she babbled something about meat and the future, she said that Julieta and Mariela were closer to Espina than any of the rest of them, they had him in their bodies, in their blood. There was a special program on the teenage cannibal soldiers of Liberia, who believe they receive the strength of the enemies they devour, and who wear necklaces made of bones. The channel that showed it was vilified as an example of shallow bad taste. Necrophilia was spoken of as the national perversion, and the cable channels programmed *Alive* and *Raw*. Even Carlitos Páez Vilaró took part in a roundtable and found himself forced to differentiate between his anthropophagy "out of necessity" and "this madness." Rock culture specialists and sociologists scrutinized the lyrics of *Meat*; some compared Espina to

Charles Manson; others, horrified, denounced their igno-
rance and simplemindedness and raised Espina to the cate-
gory of poet and visionary.

Julieta and Mariela, meanwhile, remained in their houses
in Mataderos, separated by ten blocks; they'd been forbidden
to communicate. They didn't go to school. Mariela's father
threatened the cameramen with a gun from the porch, and
the media withdrew to the corner. The neighbors did talk,
and they said the predictable things: good girls, slightly re-
bellious teenagers, what an atrocity, this can never happen
again. Many of them moved away. The girls' smiles, frozen
on their TV screens and on front pages of newspapers, terrified them.

Meanwhile, all over the country, in every internet café, the
Espinosas gathered before computer screens, because the
emails had started to come. No one could swear they were
from Julieta and Mariela—who knew if the girls even had
internet access in their isolation—but they all sensed that
they were, they wanted it to be true, and they jealously
guarded their secret. The emails spoke of two girls who would
soon turn eighteen and would be free of their parents and
doctors to play the songs of *Meat* in basements and garages.
They talked about an unstoppable underground cult, about
They Who Have Espina in their bodies. The fans waited, glit-
ter on their cheeks, their nails painted black and their lips
stained with red wine, for the message that would give them
the date and place of the second coming, the map of a forbidden land. And they listened to the last song on *Meat* (the one
where Espina whispers, "If you are hungry, eat of my flesh. If
you are thirsty, drink from my eyes"), dreaming of the future.

No Birthdays or Baptisms

He was always around, the kind of acquaintance who turned up at parties although no one knew who invited him, but I only became friends with him that summer when all my other friends decided to become assholes—otherwise known as the summer when I decided to hate all my friends.

He was different from the others. He never slept, same as me, and our nocturnal connection united us, at first by chance in desolate chat rooms at four in the morning, when our screen names always appeared, the only ones awake at that hour wanting to talk: *zedd* and *crazyjane*. He had chosen the last name of a legendary underground New York director he adored, in spite of the fact that he'd never seen a single one of the man's movies. I had chosen mine from a Yeats poem. I think we became friends just because he knew immediately who Crazy Jane was, and I knew who Zedd was.

Then we started to meet up at bars. Both of us hated the people who got drunk to the point of vomiting or acting ridiculous and making pathetic confessions, so we would sip our whiskeys slowly and criticize everyone else. I never met anyone who smoked as much as him: he'd go through three packs in one night.

Nico (Zedd's real name) had studied film for fifteen minutes and hated everything, but thanks to a preposterous job (dog walking), he'd managed to save enough money to buy a camera. That summer, he still hadn't decided what to do with it. But in one of our talks at the bar, while some awful band played (everything seemed awful to us that summer), Nico came up with a way to make money with the camera.

The following Monday his ad started to run in the newspaper. It said: "Nicolás. Weird film projects. I don't do birthdays, baptisms, or family parties. Ideal for voyeurs. I don't do anything illegal or work for cuckolds. Call . . ." I told him it wasn't likely anyone would call, or would even understand what he was trying to say with the ad. He replied that weird or disturbed people would understand. He was sure. And he was right.

He didn't tell me when he got his first jobs, but he called me as soon as he had a few videos ready. We shut ourselves in to watch them in his one-room studio, which had two bookshelves full of movies on VHS and DVD meticulously organized in alphabetical order, and a mountain of books with paragraphs underlined on every page. Any normal person would have suffocated in his apartment from all the smoke. But for every three packs he went through, I smoked two. All my efforts to cut down to ten cigarettes a day had been in vain. All my willpower had evaporated that summer, and I couldn't manage to meet goals as simple as sleeping at night and eating at least twice a day. Since I lived alone, there was no one around to point out my depression or try to cheer me up. I hadn't had such a good time in years.

Most of the videos were of couples fucking. The strange thing was that no one (or almost no one) made sure Nico didn't keep a copy. I guess that would be asking too much, and plus there was no way to be sure, and probably they didn't care. Nico explained to me that they got extra turned on by being filmed, they treated him like he was a porn director. They didn't want to film their amateur movie themselves and keep it private as a couple. They wanted someone else to do it—that was part of the excitement. He showed me a few of the videos, but they were boring. Watching people fuck is boring. Neither Nico nor I could understand why the pornography business rakes in millions.

Another video was of women in high heels walking down the street. Couldn't they find that in sex shops that sold fetish videos? Well, Nico explained, you could find women in high heels, of course, but these guys asked him to film women walking down specific streets in the city: they didn't want generic heels on anonymous walks. Another video was, precisely, a tour of the city; that was a request from a phobic girl who hadn't been able to leave her house in six months. He told me that when he gave her the film, the girl had hugged him, in tears. He'd never seen a person so pale, he said.

Now comes the most interesting one, he said then, and he placed in the tray a CD that he'd titled "Girls" in black marker. He explained that a man had hired him to film girls out in the open, in parks, in the street, on school playgrounds. He only wanted them under twelve but over six, and exclusively blond ones. Nico didn't ask why or what for, but it wasn't hard to imagine, and that's why he'd had to pretend to be sitting on a park bench with the camera on his knees, waiting, when in reality it was on and he was trying to stealthily focus on the little girls as they played. Nico didn't have a fixed price for filming (generally he negotiated with his customers), but he wasn't surprised when the presumed pedophile offered him three thousand pesos. Really, Nico became convinced the guy was a pedophile when he announced the figure he was willing to pay.

He turned in the video, he told me, and the next day the man called back, displeased. At first he didn't know or couldn't explain why, until finally, after a lot of hemming and hawing, he said only that the video didn't have enough skin. Nico replied that he thought he had the solution, and he asked the man to trust him; the guy committed to paying double if he was satisfied. We watched the video: Nico had chosen a warm-water pool at a club, a swim class for girls between six and nine years old. There were several blond ones: it was a club in Barrio Norte. Through the steam, the girls trotted along the edge of the pool, and the zoom focused in on their wet swimsuits hugging pubic areas, droplets sliding over their little asses or down between their legs. One of the girls caressed the hair of another who, in a fit of childish affection, kissed her effusively and then rested her head on her friend's shoulder. In the pool you could see kicking legs, little asses swimming away through the choppy water; at the poolside, some of the girls adjusted their suits when the straps slipped down and left their flat chests almost bare.

"Did he like it?" I wanted to know.

Nico smiled, and in reply he told me he'd received six thousand pesos, with a tip of five hundred more.

When Nico called me one terrible, freezing day while I was trying to study something tedious, I could tell from his tone that this was something urgent related to his job; it was the only thing that ever made him sound happy.

A woman had called him two days earlier, he said. She hadn't wanted to explain anything over the phone, but that didn't seem strange to him: requests for erotic videos were always like that. He went to her house with no great expectations. But right away he realized his intuition had failed him. There was something about the woman, her curved posture, her meticulous but overdone makeup that didn't hide the lack of sleep or the circles under her eyes, and above all the fact that she offered him tea. Nymphomaniacs never made tea, he explained. Always coffee, or in the evening a glass of red wine.

The woman started to explain what she wanted with almost didactic calm: Nico guessed she was a teacher, not just because of how she laid out the facts, but because in spite of how she wrung her hands and tried to hold back tears, she had looked disapprovingly at his dyed hair, and she'd paused for a second, confused, at the black polish Nico used on his nails.

Her daughter had started to hallucinate, the woman explained. Not long ago. The girl had always said that she saw things, but the mother had never believed her. She'd always been a normal girl. Shy, but normal. She didn't have many friends, but the family had moved a lot in recent years and Marcela, the daughter, hadn't had time to make friends.

They had tried psychiatric treatment with no results. The woman was desperate. The girl refused to accept that what she saw in her hallucinations wasn't real. No one had been able to convince her otherwise. So her husband had had an idea (Nico knew the bit about the husband was a lie: no man would invite a stranger in to witness the horror his daughter had become; plus, there was a reason he wasn't present for the conversation). They would film her while she was hallucinating, and that's how they would prove to her, when she saw the tape, that she was alone, screaming at the walls. It had to be VHS, because Marcela was suspicious and she wouldn't believe them if they used more modern and sophisticated formats; she would say they had manipulated the image to fool her. That was no problem, Nico had the equipment. When Nico said yes, he would do it, the woman looked at him resolutely and tried to hide her emotion. With a certain ceremoniousness, she invited him upstairs to her daughter's room.

Nico admitted he was expecting something else. A girl tied to the bed, or drugged, even a padded room. But, he said,

Marcela was wearing an enormous sweater, like a man's except it was a shade of old rose, and jeans several sizes too big. There was no telling if she was fat or thin. Her head was shaved—the wisest course of action after the prolonged and systematic yanking out of her hair that had started along with the hallucinations, the mother had explained earlier. On her cheek was a thin scar, a faint silvery line. In the room he saw a bra tossed on the bed, several dolls sitting in a row on a wooden shelf, a TV, several photos of Marcela in frames and others tacked to the wall: Marcela in the snow wearing a blue wool hat, Marcela receiving a diploma, Marcela in front of the altar, her expression frightened, at her First Communion. She wasn't hallucinating just then. When the mother excused herself and left Nico alone with her, Marcela came closer. Nico told me she was wearing a cheap and old-fashioned perfume that reminded him of aunts and mothers. She told him softly, "I know why she brought you here. You'll see it's true. I never lie." Then she smiled at him, and Nico believed it all. When, a little later, she came even closer to give him a light, Nico got a big whiff of the smell that the spinster perfume was meant to hide. It was on her hands; they stank of vaginal fluids, blood, sex, dead fish rotting in the sun.

She didn't hallucinate that day, and the mother asked Nico if he had a cellphone. Obviously, Nico did. The woman had called him on a cellphone, it was the number in the ad. She was a little overwhelmed, poor thing. In any case, what she wanted to know was if she could count on him full-time in the coming days. He promised not to take any other jobs, but he asked her for more money. We spent the next day waiting for the call together, in his studio, the phone on the bed, staring at it as if we were expecting a call from a kidnapper who had taken the person we loved most. We tried to reconstruct Marcela's story with the clues we had. Catholic school. Hallucinations since childhood. Something about religion/taboo/sex, hence the compulsive masturbation. The self-harm: I told him I thought Marcela always used long-sleeved shirts or sweaters because, just as she'd cut her face, she must be cutting her body. Marcela seemed so intense to us; I think we envied her. She was so different from everyone else, everyone we felt contempt for or fled from, those people who held no mystery, with their boring problems and their cowardice. We went back to the story the mother had told. We knew without anyone telling us that Marcela was an only child. We'd bet money she was a virgin.

The mother called Nico at seven in the evening. I knew I couldn't go with him, and I could barely stand the tension of those incredibly long three hours during which he filmed Marcela from every possible angle. Later on we watched her together, her shaved head banging against walls while she pulled off her enormous sweater (and there were scars on her arms, they looked like a map or a spiderweb), until the moment when, facedown, she stuck fingers in her vagina and ass, screaming *"Enough!"* and *"No!"* We were silent when the tape reached the end and the lines came back on the screen, gray, white, and black. Nico admitted that, for a moment, he had expected and hoped to see on the tape the thing

Marcela saw. He had believed such a thing was possible. He would have *liked* it to be possible, to be real.

Marcela refused to believe the tape showed her alone. After she saw it, the mother said, it had been very difficult to calm her down. This time, the mother didn't offer Nico any tea. She just said that Marcela wanted him to film her again and she hadn't been able to refuse, but she couldn't pay him any more. Nico said he would do it for free. The mother didn't seem sufficiently grateful.

When Nico filmed Marcela the first time, the mother had run from the room right at the moment when her daughter pulled down her pants. After the masturbation, Marcela had climbed into bed to sleep, completely naked. Her body was beautiful in spite of the scars. Nico had filmed her as she slept, and then he'd cut that part out before turning in the tape. Her sunken stomach, almost free of scars, her pointed breasts, without nipples (she'd cut them off), pulsing faintly to her heartbeat, her soft thighs covered in golden fuzz, their tautness interrupted by brutal scars that looked like seams, and the astonishing web on her arms that bore witness to their butchering.

The filmed tour of Marcela's naked body lasted over half an hour. Nico told me he would have liked to lie down beside her, but he held back. Instead, dazed, he had left the room to go find the mother. He knocked shyly on her bedroom door: through the crack he could see her lying on the double bed, facedown. The mother got up and composed herself before walking him to the door, but she didn't say a word to him, or even look him in the eyes. Nico told her he would bring the video as soon as possible, but not even then did she reply.

On the next visit it was the father who received him. I'd imagined a shy, timorous man. But Nico told me that, somehow, he'd looked more like a cop or a soldier. We were both wrong; he was just your average physical therapist. He seemed more open to conversation than his wife had been. He served coffee, and, running his hand through his graying hair, he contributed a few more valuable details, though they were surely wrong. Marcela had always had a lot of imagination, and he felt guilty for having encouraged her. She'd always played with invisible friends. But it had never been a problem until she got to high school and started to withdraw more and more, and she never wanted to go to parties, or spend the night at classmates' houses, or go dancing, much less meet boys. He said he was a modern father, he'd assumed it was a phase and let it go. After all, Marcela had always done well in school. The bigger problems had begun just a year before, and he couldn't think of any trigger, no traumatic event that would explain it. His daughter's breakdown was a mystery to him.

Neither of the parents, Nico pointed out to me, ever mentioned the mutilations or the masturbation. It was as if they were talking about a minor problem, like they'd found a marijuana cigarette on their daughter's nightstand. The second video also ended with a long discovery of Marcela's body, slender and destroyed. Same as in the first, the camera didn't record the existence of that being she claimed to see when she hallucinated.

. . .

There were no more videos, but there was another phone call. By then, Nico had pointed out Marcela's house as we drove by, a simple façade: garage, side door, and large window, brick walls and wooden details. It was the father who called: the mother, Nico thought, was having a breakdown of her own. He said his daughter didn't want another film session, but she did want to talk to Nico.

She didn't say much. She had him sit down. It was a strange day at the end of October, humid, almost hot. It was the first time Marcela hadn't worn long sleeves, and her scars were in full view. They weren't ugly: they were surprisingly symmetrical, as if she had used her skin as a canvas, or as wood she worked with a chisel. Her hair was growing out, a blond fuzz that shone under the artificial lamplight, because she never raised the blinds. The TV was still off, and the childhood photos Nico had seen before were gone.

Marcela spoke slowly and without looking at him, shy but determined, as if she had to solve an urgent and unpleasant matter. She told him he was the only person who had believed her, and that it was a shame he hadn't been able to see. She'd thought that Nico was the one, the chosen one, but she'd been wrong. She told him she didn't want to do those things to herself, but lately she couldn't help it. And she wanted to see the videos of her naked body. Nico started when he heard that, and he thought about asking her not to tell her parents. But she reassured him: It hadn't bothered her that he filmed her. She just wanted to see.

"I've never seen my body," she explained. "I shower with my eyes closed. I change clothes with my eyes closed."

"But when you cut yourself . . . ?"

"I don't cut myself. He cuts me. While I'm asleep."

Then she asked him to leave because she had something to do. Nico decided then that he was never going to give her that video to watch, and that he would never go back to that house.

We barely ever talked about Marcela again. I thought Nico had fallen in love with her, and that he was a coward for not trying to see her again, but I probably would have done the same thing. We stopped meeting up as often: being together was being with Marcela, and neither of us wanted to have her always between us, naked and ravaged. I went back to my ex-friends, but I never told them anything: one must maintain certain loyalties. I asked him once, in one of our no-longer-habitual chats, if he still had the videos. He said yes. He asked me if I wanted them. I said no. He assured me that he was going to throw them out that very night. I don't know if he did. I never asked.

Kids Who Come Back

When she started the job at the Chacabuco Park Development and Participation Center, which was just under the highway, Mechi thought she would never get used to the constant shaking above her head, a muffled sound that combined the speeding cars, the vibration of the asphalt joints, the efforts of the pillars. It seemed to throb, and Mechi sat right beneath it in a perfectly square office she shared with two other women, Graciela and Maria Laura, both employees with much more experience, both charged with attending the public, something Mechi didn't know how to do and didn't want to. But as the months passed she did start to grow accustomed to the highway over her head, and she even came to recognize different vehicles: when a large truck passed, it was like the ceiling received blows from a hammer, or like a giant were walking over the office; buses produced a slow whistle, and cars were a slight, beating hum. The rhythm of the traffic accompanied her work and gave her the feeling of being cloistered, or in an aquarium, and somehow it helped her.

Mechi's silent work kept her isolated. Her task was to maintain and update the archive of lost and disappeared children in the city of Buenos Aires, kept in the largest file cabinet in the office, which was part of the Council on the Rights of Children and Teens. Not even she was clear yet on the bureaucratic networks of councils and centers and agencies that they belonged to, and sometimes she felt hazy on who exactly she was working for; but in her ten years as a city government employee, this was the first time she had liked her job. Since she'd taken over—almost two years before— the archive had received lavish praise. And that was in spite of the fact that it had a merely documentary value: the important files, the ones that mobilized police and investigators to follow up clues about the kids, were in police departments and prosecutors' offices. Her archive was more useless, a sort of constantly expanding report without the capacity to inspire action. Although it was, on the other hand, open to the public: sometimes relatives came in to go over the archive and see if some loose thread would allow them to put together the puzzle of where their lost children were. Or they came back in to add new suspicions, new details. Among the most desperate were those referred to in the office jargon as "victims of parental kidnapping." Fathers or mothers whose spouse or partner had fled with the baby they shared. Usually, it was the mothers who ran. And the men came in often, distraught: for them, time was essential, because babies' appearances change very quickly. As soon as the first personality traits emerged, hair grew out, and eye color was defined, that baby, frozen in time in the photo on the "Missing" posters, would disappear once again.

In all the time Mechi had been in charge of the archive, no child kidnapped by a mother or father had ever reappeared.

Luckily, she didn't have to look the missing children's families in the face. When they came into the office, if they wanted to see their file, Graciela or Maria Laura asked Mechi for it and then they would hand it over to the relatives. The system was the same if people came in to give new information: they left it with or told it to one of the other two women, who then passed it on to Mechi, and she added it to the correct file—or rather files, one digital and the other paper. Sometimes, especially when Graciela and Maria Laura got caught up in their long personal conversations, or went out to eat and took their time coming back, Mechi opened the files and daydreamed about the children. She even had a separate file cabinet where she kept the solved cases, those of the kids who had reappeared. The ones who were found were almost always teenagers and usually girls: kids who'd said they were going out dancing, and then didn't come back. Jessica, for example. She lived on the corner of Piedrabuena and Chilavert, in Villa Lugano. The house shown in the photos was squat and had a dirty white façade. It didn't advertise what went on inside. Six kids, a single mother, and Jessica's room, bare walls of unfinished bricks, a foam mattress over boards (tech-

nically, she didn't have a bed), and her section of the wall—
because she shared the room with two siblings—decorated
with photos of Guille, her hero. Pictures of Guille torn from
magazines, or more or less whole posters, covered in pink
kisses, and "I love yous" written in red marker. Jessica always
met up with other girls in Plaza Sudamérica, recently refitted
with new iron benches (so it would be uncomfortable to sit
for very long, or, even worse, sleep on them) and police
guards. People said she wasn't a troublemaker, she'd never
even been caught smoking a cigarette. But one day she ran
away, and her desperate family went out to search the neighborhood and put up flyers; they made sure to leave the photo-
copies of Jessica's picture at all the taxi stands, because taxi
drivers know everyone. Jessica reappeared two months later:
she'd been staying at a friend's house after an argument with
her mom, who had yelled at her, "If you keep this up, I'll ship
you off to Comodoro Rivadavia." That was where Jessica's father lived. When the girl reappeared, Mechi sat looking at
her photo—her hair dyed a deep shade of red, her lips
glossed, and earrings shaped like music clefs—and she
thought she should tell the kid—Jessica was fourteen years
old—that surely Comodoro Rivadavia was much better than
Villa Lugano, and maybe her dad would get her a bed that
didn't look like a giant sponge. But Jessica wanted to stay in
Buenos Aires so she could go to all of Guille's concerts there;
Guille never went to Patagonia.

There were many Jessicas, because most of the missing
kids were teenage girls. They took off with an older guy, or
got scared by a pregnancy. They fled from a drunken father,
from a stepfather who raped them in the early morning, from

a brother who masturbated onto their backs at night. They went out to the club and got drunk and lost a couple of days, and then were afraid to come home. There were also the crazy girls, who heard something snap in their heads the day they decided to go off their medications. And the ones who were taken, the kidnapped girls who disappeared in prostitution rings, never to resurface, or to resurface dead, or as murderers of their captors, or as suicide victims on the Paraguayan border, or dismembered in a Mar del Plata hotel.

. . .

Mechi thought her meticulousness in maintaining the archive, her serious interest in the missing kids, must be connected to Pedro, one of her few friends. She had met him about five years before, when she was still working right downtown in an office near Plaza de Mayo. She'd get distracted looking out the window at the marches and protests, and practically her only entertainment—her only strong emotion—came when some manifestation ended in repression, and the sirens, screams, and the burning smell of tear gas reached her window. Some afternoons Mechi decided to have a beer before going back to her apartment. She didn't much care for any of the bars in the area. At the end of the day, around six in the evening, they filled up with young executives, well-paid administrative employees, and secretaries in expensive clothes, who all went to happy hours and ordered imported beers and tried to call attention to themselves, to meet each other, and, if possible, take someone they liked to bed. No one tried to talk to Mechi. She was too skinny and short, she wore platform boots in summer, and she never wore makeup. She was weird. Nor did she expect any of the clean-shaven guys wearing suits and cologne to treat her to an Iguana beer; Mechi easily accepted the reality of a situation, and wasn't one to agonize over it. Those bars weren't her place. But she liked to get home a little buzzed, to walk down the avenue while the sun sank and it became very easy to ignore what went on around her. Sometimes she even brought a book to the bar, and that attracted some glances, but no one had ever bothered to ask what she was reading. With a book, she could tune out the conversations of the other office workers, which didn't interest her at all.

One of those evenings she met Pedro, who pulled her from her isolation when he asked if he could share the table—the bar was full. He talked a lot, with no need for her to ask any questions: he told her he was a journalist, that he worked at a nearby newspaper, that he was a police reporter and that he rarely left the newsroom to drink a beer in the evening (he left work after ten at night), but that day had been particularly hectic and he'd needed to clear his mind. He asked for her number and Mechi gave it to him without much expectation: Pedro was nervous, attractive, with a five o'clock shadow and big, dark eyes. That kind of guy rarely noticed her.

But Pedro called the next night. He invited her for a beer at another bar, different, cheaper, and far from the office workers' circuit, and later on to drink more at his apartment. Mechi still remembered the place, the litter box in the laundry room beside the kitchen overflowing with shit; he must not have cleaned it in weeks. Books in the corners, a beautiful stone balcony, the computer on the table, and a vintage poster of the Al Pacino film *Dog Day Afternoon*. They sipped their beers sitting on the sofa and went to bed before they'd finished them. Bed was a mattress on the floor, with the alarm clock to one side, a full ashtray within arm's reach, and the white sheets overly used, so much so that in the center they looked gray. Mechi hadn't enjoyed the sex with Pedro. For some reason she'd been unable to concentrate, and she spent the whole time looking at the decorative details on the closet doors, the night sky, the cat's curious eyes peering in through the cracked door, even the lit window of the apartment across the street, which she could see from the bed. She'd acted like she enjoyed it because Pedro seemed to be having fun, and she'd reacted with enthusiasm and delicacy when necessary. She'd kissed him deeply and caressed his back, but when he reached for a second condom, Mechi gently stopped him, kissed his cheek, and asked for a cigarette. They stayed up smoking until dawn. Pedro did a little cocaine— she didn't feel like it—and told her details of some of the most lurid cases he'd covered. He told Mechi that he liked it that she didn't get disgusted by the details, that she was never shocked. She explained that crime stories did frighten her, but they also entertained her. She left Pedro's apartment as the sun was coming up, sure that they wouldn't have sex again. And she wasn't wrong there, but she misjudged Pedro when she thought that they would never talk again either. Pedro wanted to keep seeing her, though he didn't try to sleep with her. That first night something had become clear that they didn't want to say out loud: they weren't attracted to each other, they'd known it even before going to bed together, but they still wanted to try, because they were alone and they'd both fantasized that the encounter could be, at least, the start of a companionship. Quite simply, they hadn't fallen in love, but they had begun a friendship that was consistent even if it wasn't all that close. At first Mechi called him to comment on his articles, and he called her to inform her of the outcome of cases she was interested in. Over the years, they confided in each other about frustrated relationships and small hopes that in general vanished quickly. Pedro changed girlfriends often; Mechi was more solitary. And although they complained, they both knew they preferred being alone.

In recent years, Pedro's police beat had changed. Tired and a little frightened after years of Mafia crimes, he'd started to investigate teen disappearances, especially girls. He ended up discovering networks trafficking in minors, and characters every bit as sordid and fearful as any narco murderer. But there was something in the terrible journeys of these girls—mostly girls, though he also investigated cases of missing boys—that led him to write special-feature essays, long and detailed, that were much commented on and brought congratulations from his bosses, and even salary raises.

Almost like a strange coincidence, while Pedro was insinuating himself into provincial brothels and dark police stations in search of the missing kids, Mechi was offered the job in the council's archive of disappeared children. She accepted immediately, and the first thing she did after saying yes and finishing the bureaucracy to make the change official was call Pedro, who received the news of Mechi's new job with shouts of joy and "I can't believe it" repeated so many times it disturbed her. He started to visit her often, and when the archive finally had the seal of Mechi's order and dedication, she became an obligatory consultation for him. Before Mechi, the archive was a pile of messy papers that no one paid much attention to, except for the poor, desperate families. In three months, according to Pedro, she'd turned it into a treasure.

"Girl, this thing is worth its weight in gold," he always told her, as he turned the pages and copied details into his notebook. "I always talk about you to the prosecutor. You'll have to meet her, she's a dyke who smokes black tobacco, she's got a voice like a dude's and a really bad dye job, you have no idea! One of these days we'll have breakfast together, okay?"

That meeting never happened—Pedro was never awake at breakfast time, and plus, he traveled at least every fifteen days to go after kidnappers of teen girls. With help from Mechi's archive and Pedro's investigations, the police had already caught one of the czars who trafficked in women and teens: a missionary settled in Posadas, where he had several open escape routes to Brazil and Paraguay, and whose tentacles reached to the southern edge of Greater Buenos Aires. He was brought to court and the terrifying details were published, and some of the girls were interviewed—several had lived right in Palermo, crammed into a one-room apartment. They weren't allowed to go outside; a woman watched over them and brought them food and essential items, and they had pale skin and cracked lips from the confinement. Pedro became a TV star, and he took part in panels, news shows, even went on cable access programs. He bought a few jackets and white shirts for his peak of stardom, and Mechi thought how easy fame and TV were for men, they just showed up in different jackets and their elegance was guaranteed; if it had been her, she would have had to buy twelve different dresses and accessories to match. Pedro was sincere and generous in interviews, and he mentioned Mechi several times, because he had deciphered much of the prostitution ring by cross-checking information, and the archives of the Council on the Rights of Children and Teens had been key. But no one had called Mechi in to talk about her kids on TV, she'd just been interviewed for a few newspaper articles. She'd received some of the journalists at the Chacabuco Park office, and they all commented on the noise of the highway that monotonously filled the office. Mechi told them that after a while you stopped hearing it, but that wasn't true, and they didn't believe her, she could tell from their false smiles. "At least you've got the park nearby," they said, and Mechi had to admit that was indeed a compensation for the racket of the highway overhead. Sometimes she took her lunch hour there: she'd quickly eat a sandwich sitting on a bench, or at a café if she hadn't brought lunch, and then she walked for a while. She especially liked the part near the subway station, a small, romantic rose garden with benches, gazebos, and pathways, whose elegant decadence was ruined only by the highway's constantly passing cars and its horrible, eraser-shaped pillars. Sometimes she brought files with her to go over the names and circumstances of the kids, mentally filling in the ellipses by inventing stories for them. She found it strange that the photo the family chose, usually the same one used for posters and flyers in the search, was almost always terrible. The kids looked ugly; the camera took in their features from so close up they looked deformed, or from so far away they were

blurred. They wore strange expressions under erratic lighting; she almost never saw photos where the missing kids
looked good.

Except for Vanadis. Vanadis, such a strange name. Mechi
had looked it up in an encyclopedic dictionary: it was a varia-
tion on the name of the Norse goddess Freya, deity of youth,
love, and beauty, and also the goddess of death. Vanadis,
who'd disappeared at fourteen years old, was almost the only
real beauty in the whole archive. There were more than
twenty photos of her, many more than usual, and in all of
them she was a mystery of dark hair and almond eyes, high
cheekbones and lips pursed in an expression of immature
seduction. Mechi had never gotten obsessed with any of the
kids, but with Vanadis she came close. Also, there was something about her story that didn't fit. They'd found her turning tricks on the transvestites' turf in Constitución, where no
women usually worked, especially not young girls. No one in
her family wanted to take her in when the social workers
intervened, and she'd been sent to a reform school, which she
ran away from. Nothing more was ever heard from her. The
family didn't seem too interested in finding her. Her street
friends did sometimes turn up with information. Other kids
who idolized her, street vendors, taxi drivers who started
their shifts in the early morning, young people who worked
at the twenty-four-hour hot dog and hamburger joints, kiosk
workers, other prostitutes, a few transvestites. Some of them
came into the office and talked about Vanadis, but others
dropped off letters, small, handwritten anecdotes, even cut-
out hearts or red ribbons to give her if she ever reappeared.
Graciela recorded many of them, and then passed on the

cassette—there was no way to get her to understand how an MP3 worked—to Mechi, who transcribed them. Those voices later stayed with her on the subway home. Vanadis's file was thick and hard to close. So much so that one afternoon, at lunchtime, one of the photos fell out near the Emilio Mitre station. When she ran after it—it was windy and she was afraid it would fly away—she saw that face on the sidewalk for an instant, and she thought that nothing bad could have happened to Vanadis, the girl who looked like Bianca Jagger but had been born in Dock Sud. Because nothing bad ever happened to goddesses, not even when they were so sad and streetwise.

. . .

When Vanadis used to turn tricks near Constitución, she'd sometimes run into the kids from the prison. Not inmates: these were kids, boys and girls—and a few adults as well—who squatted in the ruins of the Caseros Prison. Those walls were supposed to have been demolished years ago, but there they remained, towering and dangerous, and no one seemed to care except the neighbors. Little by little it had filled up with addict kids, usually hooked on cocaine paste, but also on glue and alcohol. The kids had run off the poor families and homeless people who had settled in the ruins. No one else could live where the addict kids lived. There were fights, overdose deaths, dealers who murdered and were murdered, theft, an abysmal squalor. No one dared walk close by the prison, and the neighborhood around the ruins slowly died.

The addict kids usually emerged from the prison at dusk and went out to panhandle nearby.

A girl from the Caseros Death House—one TV station had referred to the ruins that way, and the macabre name stuck—came in one day to the Chacabuco Park Development and Participation Center and said she wanted to report what she knew about Vanadis. She didn't want to go to the police or the judge, she told Graciela, because she was in too deep and didn't want to go to jail or rehabilitation—she wanted to die in the street, she didn't care about anything. Her arms and legs were covered in sores, and she'd lost two pregnancies in the Caseros ruins; she didn't know who the fathers of her unborn children were, she figured they must have been other addicts, but she didn't remember. And she surely must have slept with them for money or more drugs, because she liked girls. She didn't want to give her name in her testimony, and she asked to just be called Loli. Graciela said that Loli stank, her clothes were so dirty that her jeans and shirt both looked brown, and her toes were poking out of her sneakers. She said Loli was so skinny there was something wolfish about her, with her teeth and jaw jutting out of her face like an animal's maw. And that the girl had told her own life story before telling about Vanadis—Loli never stopped talking, or only to take in breath with a guttural sound. It was the first time Graciela had seen a moribund person walking, a person whose mind didn't register the death of the body. She'd been shocked.

Loli told about how one night she had gone out of the Death House, desperate. She didn't have a cent to her name, everything hurt, she couldn't think, she needed money. She went along the side of Constitución Station, but carefully, because she didn't want any cops to see her, and she didn't want to ask the trannies for money, because they beat up girls like her. She had to find someone who was waiting for the bus, or just walking along, going to the kiosk or back home. She had the broken neck of a bottle hidden in her jacket pocket.

About an hour passed, she thought, and she didn't come across a single person she could mug. Regular people no longer walked around the neighborhood at that hour, they knew it got dangerous. And just when she was losing all hope, she saw Vanadis. Loli was out of her mind, but right away she knew this was no tranny. She went up behind her and pressed the sharp edge of the bottle into her back. Vanadis turned around very fast, almost with a jump—she was much more alert than Loli had thought. They looked at each other, and Vanadis ceded without any need to threaten her again. She gave Loli thirty pesos and told her, "But now you can't ask for more for fifteen days, okay? Don't bust my balls. Remember I gave you money, don't be lame."

Loli ran off with the money and a strange feeling: it was as if she hadn't robbed that girl. If the girl had said she wouldn't give her anything, Loli would have left without pushing further. She didn't understand why, when she was so desperate for money, but that's how it was: she would have left her alone.

Some days later—Loli didn't know exactly how long, time didn't count for the people of the Death House—she saw her again. Vanadis told her, "Don't even think about it. You remember, right?" Loli did remember, and when Vanadis smiled at her, she fell in love. She asked if she could stick around, and Vanadis said yes. Loli told her story, talked about the Death House, and Vanadis got worried. She didn't do drugs herself, she found their effect so sad. She told Loli she wanted to see it, wanted to visit the Death House, but Loli refused to take her. It was too dangerous, and plus she didn't want Vanadis to see the awful place where she lived. Those nights, when they smoked cigarettes together between Vanadis's customers, Loli thought she could get off drugs, start eating again, go to the free hospital to cure everything that had surely gone to shit in her body, and confess her love. Maybe Vanadis would love her back—there were loads of lesbo whores, she'd met a ton of them and she'd even had a hooker girlfriend back before she started smoking paco.

Loli told Graciela that Vanadis worked a lot. No doubt she took customers away from the trannies, but for some reason they let her work in peace, no one bothered her. Loli never even saw the johns—they were always inside a car and it was always night. Vanadis didn't talk about them either—in general she talked very little and almost never about herself; she never mentioned her family, her home, nothing that came before her life in the street. If Loli asked her, Vanadis just smiled and changed the subject. But she had told Loli about one pair of johns who were "weird." That's what Loli wanted to come in and report: because when Vanadis ran away from the reform school and disappeared, she thought maybe those weird guys had taken her. Plus, when Loli found out that Vanadis had disappeared—one of the trannies told her—she realized she was never going to quit paco and that she was going to die in Caseros. Vanadis had been her last door out, and it was closed now. Loli wanted to tell what she knew so her death wouldn't be so futile.

The weird guys picked Vanadis up together and brought her to a hotel nearby, almost right across from the station. While one of them fucked her the other one filmed, and they took turns. They made her do normal things: suck dick, take it up the ass, regular sex. But they filmed her. Vanadis had asked them what they did with the videos and the guys said they were just for personal use, they weren't doing anything strange. Vanadis didn't believe them, and Loli didn't either. When Vanadis kept insisting they tell her where the videos would end up, online or what, they told her that if she said anything they'd kill her, that she was nothing but a street kid, and who in the world would give a fuck about her. Vanadis didn't argue, and she kept doing the videos, but she was afraid of those men. She wouldn't admit it but Loli could tell, even though Vanadis always denied it, saying they were just a couple of assholes, and anyway she didn't care if they put her videos online or sold them, it was all the same to her. The men, of course, paid more than the usual customers, and that was enough for her.

Loli hadn't learned that the social workers and police had come to Constitución until after Vanadis was sent to reform school. She hoped she'd come back, and after a really long time—it seemed like years—the tranny told her Vanadis had disappeared. And that just killed her, said Loli, it killed me. Maybe they'd killed her too. That girl was beautiful, the most beautiful thing I've seen in my life.

Everyone agreed that Vanadis was beautiful, especially on her MySpace page; it was remarkable how many of the disappeared kids left Facebook and MySpace profiles behind. They sat immobile, like headstones, visited only by a handful of the kids' hundreds of friends and a few family members who went on leaving messages with the hope of one day receiving an answer.

Vanadis's profile had surprised Mechi. It had new messages almost every day. There wasn't much information about her, though. An extraordinary photo, taken with a cellphone: she had her hair pulled back very tight and you could see her whole face, her full lips in a soft smile. She'd completed the information requested with a strange mixture of truth and macabre fantasy: she was a fan of heavy metal and horror movies. She called herself "Vagabond of the Night," described herself as "the worm that lives in every death," and claimed to be 103 years old. She'd left the space for "About me" blank, and for "Who I want to meet," she'd put "Everyone."

The rest went like this:

INTERESTS

General: No time now, I'll finish later
Music: metal!!!
Movies: saw, the exorcist, the others, japanese movies
TV: I don't have one it's bad for you!!!
Books: haha
Heroes: my fingers
Groups: marilyn manson, slipknot, korn
Status: None
I'm here for: friends

Orientation: bisexual

Hometown: the underworld

Measurements: 5 foot 2, super skinny!!!

Ethnicity: ?

Religion: nothing

Sign: scorpio

Drink/smoke: yes and yes

Children: poor kids

Schooling: ?

Salary: haha

She had 228 friends and 7,200 messages. "hope you come back pretty girl i luv you!" "hey beautiful, I love you come back you are missed." Some of her friends had profiles of their own, but not many had filled them out. Except for Negative Zero, a tattoo artist who had an extensive profile full of photos of his work, including several of Vanadis: he had tattooed two wings over her shoulder blades and a tear on the nape of her neck—or at least, those were the tattoos of hers that he displayed. But he left messages at least once a week on Vanadis's profile: some of them were short ("tell me where you are dollface," "if anyone hurt you I'll kill them"), and others very long, up to the limit of words allowed for one message: "witch girl, I'll never forget you or what you told me, I looked for you last night everywhere in constitución and in patricios I even went into the prison and almost got mugged if you started smoking that shit I'll beat your ass but I'll save you ok, tell me where you are I feel like you're not dead the other night you came to me in a dream you floated above my bed I was naked face up and you were floating with real wings like the ones I gave you and your eyes were weird and silvery, it made me remember when you came here and told me you had to sleep under covers even if it was hot because you felt like hands touched you during the night, you had some really fucking crazy dreams and sometimes you heard voices whispering in your ear that wouldn't let you sleep, I looked for you in the hospitals too, have you gone crazy out there? Sometimes you seemed really crazy my love I went to open door and to the moyano but you're not anywhere I'm gonna go crazy."

Mechi gave Graciela the guy's name and asked if he'd ever come in to give information, but no, she'd never seen him. Mechi believed him, he seemed truly in love, and she felt so sorry for him that sometimes she thought about breaking her promise not to get involved with the kids beyond the archive. She wanted to go see the tattoo artist and ask him to tell her more about those dreams and those voices, but in the end she decided to keep her distance. The special attention she paid Vanadis seemed unfair to the other kids, and she decided, as always, to leave the matter alone.

. . .

It had been a year since that sensational case of the missionary who ran a child prostitution ring, and except for the individual successes of a few girls who reappeared (mostly girls—Mechi was amazed, so many girls), the office went on with its usual rhythm, distressing but routine. Pedro had gone back to his maps marked with the movement of the kidnapped girls: he often followed their trails thanks to inscriptions that they themselves left in bathrooms of gas stations and hotels: "It's Daiana, I'm alive mom I'm kidnapped I love you help." Every fifteen or twenty days he visited Mechi and her archive. He took notes, and when Graciela wasn't looking he photocopied the pages he needed. Mechi, though, preferred to meet up with him at the bar. It was uncomfortable at the office because Pedro shouted all the time, even more after he'd had a few beers. He'd already been a little like that when they first met, excitable, chain-smoking, answering the phone nonstop. But these days he drank too much and got drunk quickly. It embarrassed Mechi, and she felt a little disgusted at the sight of the saliva droplets flying out of Pedro's mouth with every peal of laughter. But sometimes he made her laugh too. And she liked to sit in the grass in the park and drink a beer with him, as if they were a couple of teenagers, while they talked about the reasons behind all those ugly photos, or how many taxi drivers ran off with minors, or if the kidnapped kids were smuggled out of the country through Paraguay (as the child welfare advocate said), or through Brazil, as the NGO investigators and the journalists suspected.

Things went on pretty much the same, until one day Pedro turned up with a tip that he called "fabulous." One of his "sources"—he never fully explained to Mechi who his informants were—was selling a video with an underage girl who'd been reported missing. She'd been filmed with a cellphone: the girl was wrapped in a blanket, or tucked in a sleeping bag or something like that, and presumably was supposed to remain hidden. The girl was dead, and what happened in the cellphone video was that, in a clumsy movement while they were carrying her out a door to load her into a truck, the wrapping fell and you could see her uncovered face perfectly. Pedro was going to pay for that video, and what he asked from Mechi was to be able to check her archive afterward to try to place the girl from the video. In Pedro's voice Mechi heard the same eager exhilaration he'd had when he was investigating the missionary case. She said yes, that after he watched the video—she absolutely didn't want to see it herself, though Pedro offered her a copy—he should come to the office and check the archive. Pedro called at the end of the day one Monday, and he arrived agitated, smelling of subway and with droplets of sweat on his forehead, as if it were summer and not August in Buenos Aires.

"How's it going, Mechita my dear. The video's really intense. It looks like shit, all pixelated, and it doesn't help me at all, because you can't see the plates on the truck they put the girl into, all the guys have their faces covered like with ski masks, the house could be any house and the street is just any awful street in Greater Buenos Aires, it could be anywhere. But you can see the girl perfectly. They toss her around like they want to show her; I don't know if the guy with the phone films her on purpose, because there's no audio, but they move her a little from here to there, the blanket falls and you can see her whole face. Then it's like a close-up, the sick sons of bitches, and one arm falls, really floppy, like this, across her chest."

"Is she dead?"

"She looks bad, but she's not stiff, and her face isn't beaten up. She could be high, drunk, asleep. I think I got ripped off.

But yeah, she could also be dead. The video lasts thirty seconds, and you can see her face for about ten, there's no way to know. A divine kid, that's for sure. Beautiful, she looks like a model."

Mechi felt herself start to sweat now too, felt her stomach harden and her cheeks burn, like when she realized she was stupidly crossing a street on a red light because she was wearing headphones and not paying attention. She hadn't told Pedro about her obsession with Vanadis. She didn't want to ask herself why, but she knew she felt ashamed, or guilty. So now, she couldn't show him how sure she was and how much it affected her. She turned around so Pedro couldn't see her face as she pulled out Vanadis's file, opened it, and asked Pedro if that was the girl. "It's her," he replied without hesitation, and he dove into the file, saying it was one of the bulkiest he'd seen. But after turning three pages, he looked up.

"How'd you know this was the girl from the video? I mean, you didn't doubt for a second, you handed me the file immediately!"

"It's a coincidence."

"What's a coincidence? Mechi, don't act all mysterious, girl, tell me."

"I was looking through that file the other day, sometimes I get bored. . . . And, well, I'd just read one of the interviews in there, with a street friend of Vanadis's—the girl's name is Vanadis—where she talks about how two guys filmed her, two of her johns. It's all there, the girl turned tricks in Constitución."

Pedro was somewhere between openmouthed and contented. Who's the friend? he wanted to know, and then Mechi told him about the Caseros ex-prison. Pedro seemed ever more pleased, and she felt a twinge of anger as always when her friend got excited at the opportunity for a new investigation that would help his career. And this one was unbeatable: the Death House, the lesbian addict, the beautiful teen who liked zombies. Mechi let her bad mood dissipate: she knew it was impossible to ask any other reaction of Pedro. Then she gave him the MySpace address, told him about the tattoo artist, and, after he begged for a couple minutes, she let him photocopy Vanadis's whole file, start to finish; they stayed after closing time to do it, as the cars passed overhead and night fell outside. Before leaving, Pedro asked her one more time if she wanted to see the video. She said no, and she also told him, with what remained of her anger, that he should bring it to the prosecutor the next morning. But he wasn't so sure. He knew it wasn't right to keep it, but he wanted to investigate more. Plus, he had so much material now. The video alone proved almost nothing, but if he got more information—which he planned to, from his informant and maybe some of Vanadis's friends, if he could track them down from the file—he could put together a better article and offer something more solid to the prosecutor. Mechi listened to his justifications without a word. She thought it was wrong for Pedro not to turn the video over to the authorities immediately, it was what he should do. But she couldn't pretend to be some kind of pure soul: she really did want to see that cellphone video, she was dying to see it, and that morbid curiosity wasn't exactly a paragon of virtue. Pedro didn't repeat his offer to show her, and she didn't ask him to see it, either. She could hold out. Pedro said goodbye with a kiss on the cheek at the subway stairs; he'd call her the next day. His plan was to look for Loli in the ruins of the Caseros prison in the early evening, then chat with some of the transvestites who would only come out to work once the sun went down, and maybe he'd even contact the infatuated tattoo artist. She said she'd wait for his call the next night, that she always left her phone on. But that night she turned it off and also disconnected the landline, so she could sleep better. It didn't work: she woke with a start several times, her chest sweating. In the morning over coffee, she couldn't remember what her nightmares were about, but she did vaguely recall the figure of a naked girl whose back was covered in blood, a kind of little angel whose wings had been torn off.

. . .

Mechi was anxious all morning, glancing sideways at her cellphone even though she wasn't expecting Pedro's call until that night. She went out for lunch a little earlier than usual, and she decided to go to a bar that was on the other side of the park for a change, to distract herself. But she never made it there. When she was going up the steps of Chacabuco Park's main fountain, which wasn't turned on that day, Mechi saw Vanadis sitting on one of the steps. No doubt about it. It was her, dressed the same as in one of the photos on her MySpace page, the only one that showed her whole body. That was precisely why Mechi recognized her, because of her clothes: it was like seeing the photo brought to life. The medium-length boots, the denim skirt, the black tights, the dark, heavy hair. She thought she must be imagining things, but it was just a passing thought, because she was absolutely sure, the nausea in her stomach and her shaking hands made that clear. She approached slowly: Vanadis didn't look at her. Finally, she planted herself right in front of the girl, so she'd have to pay attention.

"Vanadis? Are you Vanadis?"

"Yeah, hi, what's up?" replied the girl, who was clearly not dead, who couldn't be the girl in the video Pedro had bought, because here she was smiling in the sun and very much alive. Her smile displayed crooked, yellow teeth, the only thing that disturbed her beauty; Mechi had never seen them in photos, perhaps because Vanadis didn't laugh much and rarely opened her mouth.

Mechi didn't know what to say. The girl didn't speak to her. She was afraid Vanadis would stand up and leave, that she'd slip through her fingers. So she asked Vanadis to please come with her, and the girl complied. She couldn't question her in their first meeting, she just made sure the girl followed her to the office, where they were met by howls of delight and surprise from Graciela and Maria Laura, who went mad with joy when they found out who this girl was. They offered Vanadis a cappuccino from the machine, and they did see fit to hound her with questions that she answered mostly with inclinations of her head and a lot of "I don't remembers." "She's in shock," said Graciela as she dialed the prosecutor and then Vanadis's mother. In twenty minutes the office was jam-packed, and Vanadis's family were all fainting, sobbing, and shouting in a reunion of demential celebration. Strange, thought Mechi, because during the whole year Vanadis was missing they never even called, and before that, when she was at reform school, they didn't visit her. Not to mention the fact that they hadn't gotten her off the street when she was turning tricks at fourteen years old. She mentioned this to Graciela, who looked at her with an expression that said, *Well, aren't you ignorant and soulless.* Then she said, didactically: "People react to trauma and loss in different ways. Some families get obsessed and never stop searching; others act like nothing happened. That doesn't mean they don't love their kids." Graciela, always with her style of permanently indignant social psychologist, and her simple but arrogant explanations. Once again, Mechi was glad that she worked separately from the other two women, that she'd never tried to make friends with them, and especially that she wasn't one of the poor family members who had to sit across from Graciela and listen to her talk.

In all the commotion, she forgot to call Pedro. She finally did it once Vanadis and her family drove off toward the courthouse to file what they needed to for the case.

"You can't even guess what happened," Mechi told him.

"Ha! You can't guess what happened here. I couldn't go to Constitución to see about Vanadis, or to the prison or anything. My editor called me all worked up to send me here. . . ."

"Where's here? Wait, Pedro, this is more—"

"I'm at Rivadavia Park, in Caballito. A woman recognized a disappeared kid, he was looking at movies at one of the stalls. A certain Juan Miguel González, thirteen years old . . ."

"Pedro, why—"

"No, let me finish, this is insane! I can't believe you haven't heard."

"Over here we've got—"

"Wait! So the woman goes up to the kid, she knew him from before, and she says, 'Juan Miguel, is that you?' And the kid says yes. Then the woman calls the family on the phone, from right there in the park, and the kid's mother starts screaming, saying they already found her son, but they found him dead, three months ago! You remember this case? It was famous, it was on TV, a total mess! The one with the kid who fell under the train. Listen to this: The mother didn't want to come see the kid who turned up in the park, she had a panic attack. The father was tougher, and he came. They had the kid at the police station, by the way, that's where my editor sent me, the cops called him directly. So the father comes, and he says it's his kid! My head is spinning and I'm not going to lie to you, I'm scared shitless, I mean shitless, that kid was dead, the train cut off his legs but didn't touch his face, it's the same face, the same kid."

"Pedro—"

"And on top of the video I saw yesterday, this is all insane!"

"Pedro, we found Vanadis, she was here, in Chacabuco Park."

"Say what?"

"Vanadis, the girl from the video."

"I know who Vanadis is, woman, especially with that weird-as-shit name! What do you mean you found her?"

"I was the one who found her, on some steps in the park, the ones near the fountain."

"You're fucking with me."

"Why would I fuck with you, don't be an ass."

"Where is she now?"

"They went to the courthouse, she's with her family."

"And it's her?"

"Yeah. She's seems a little weird, but it's her."

"It can't be, it can't be. Wait, I'm getting another call, let me call you back, are you gonna be there?"

. . .

In the following weeks things reached an unprecedented level of hysteria, and then got a little worse. Kids who'd gone missing from their houses began to turn up, but not just anywhere: they appeared in one of four of the city's parks, Chacabuco, Avellaneda, Sarmiento, and Rivadavia. They stayed there, sleeping at night one beside another, and they seemed to have no intention of going anywhere. There were even babies, presumably those victims of parental kidnapping, though they could have also been stolen from hospital maternity wards. Their frantic families came to get them without thinking too much about how odd the case was, how unsettling it was that the children should come back all at the same time. The first ones to leave the parks were, obviously, the babies. Among the older kids, silence reigned. None of them said much, or seemed to want to talk about where they had been. Nor did they seem to recognize their families, though they left with the people who came to pick them up with a meekness that was somehow even more disturbing.

No one else knew what to say, either, and crazy theories started to fly. Since the kids wouldn't talk, it couldn't be proven that some criminal organization had set them all free at once, for example, but that was the claim a few newspapers put forth. There were even police raids, and people were arrested as they shouted their innocence into the cameras—most likely they were telling the truth. There was no evidence to support charging them with anything in the case of the returned kids. But not many of the investigators, functionaries, and journalists had the honesty of Mechi or Pedro, who sincerely had no idea what was happening and couldn't explain it; they only knew that they were very afraid.

After the euphoric bewilderment of the first week, a chill began to spread. It turned out that the "recovered" kids of that first week were the normal cases. Except, of course, for the case of Juan Miguel, the boy who'd been hit by a train. The media had decided that Juan Miguel's mother and father were poor drunks, and as such they were unreliable: they'd identified the wrong kid. The public accepted that story with relief. For the rest of that first week, then, everything happened relatively normally: boys and girls who had disappeared recently, from more or less stable families, with no signs of violence. Practically happy endings. But toward the middle of the second week, a muffled dread started to settle in that no one dared put into words for fear that their echoes would never end. One of its triggers was the case of Victoria Caride. An economics student, one of the few upper-middle-class kids who'd disappeared. It was said she could have been kidnapped by human traffickers, or suffered a psychotic break when she stopped taking her antidepressants, or else she'd taken off with a married man. Victoria's case was a mystery, in sum, a girl who had gone out to buy cookies and never come back; a meticulous girl, with friends, money, university studies, and moral scruples that she channeled into volunteer work at a soup kitchen. It had been five years since she'd disappeared, and almost no hope of finding her remained. But now she'd appeared in Avellaneda Park, near the station of the decrepit little train that wound around the property; she was sitting on a bench and looking off toward the mansion that had once been an estate house. Her family was elated, and no sooner did they see her on TV—there was a mobile news unit in every park, day and night—than they came for her and whisked her away, squeezing her in an embrace of tears and runny noses.

At first, neither Victoria's family nor anyone else dared to mention that the girl had not changed at all, physically speaking, in the five years she'd been gone. She was wearing the same clothes she had on the day she disappeared, even the same clip holding her curly brown hair back in a ponytail.

The second case was even trickier to explain: Lorena López, a girl from Villa Soldati who had run away from home with a taxi driver, and had been five months pregnant when she left. She appeared in the rose garden at Chacabuco Park, five months pregnant. She'd been missing for a year and a half. The gynecologists confirmed that it was her first pregnancy. And so? She must not have been pregnant when she left, it must have been a mistake, or maybe the girl had lied—the taxi driver didn't turn up to confirm or deny anything, and well he didn't, because he would have gone straight to jail for statutory rape. Or maybe the doctors were wrong—how could they be so sure? Lorena went back to Soldati, but after fifteen days her family "returned her" to the corresponding juvenile court. Pedro had seen them hand her over. He told Mechi how the mother had said to the judge, "I don't know who this girl is, but she is not my daughter. I was wrong. She looks a lot like her, but she's not my daughter. I gave birth to Lorena. I would recognize her in the dark, just from her smell. And this is not my daughter." The judge ordered a DNA test, and they were still waiting for the results when another missing boy appeared, chatting with other kids under the Bolivar monument in Rivadavia Park. He was one of the most famous runaways, nicknamed Buckaroo or Super Buckaroo, real name Jonathan Ledesma. Buckaroo was a chronic runaway and a little thief in the making: at twelve years old he had fled his house in Pompeya ten times, and broken out of two reform schools. People saw him everywhere, because Buckaroo went out in the streets and picked pockets at the Avenida 9 de Julio stoplight, but no one had managed to keep track of him long enough to catch him. Plus, long periods of time passed when absolutely nothing was known of his whereabouts.

Buckaroo's case, however, was closed. A year before, he'd been run over by a bus on La Noria Bridge. He'd gotten dizzy while snatching purses and collapsed onto the road. The truck's wheels rolled right over his chest and he couldn't be saved. But his face had been left intact, same as Juan Miguel's, the boy from the train. And it was the same as the face in the photos, the same as this Buckaroo who was in Rivadavia Park. Only it was impossible for Buckaroo to be there with the other reappeared children, because Buckaroo was dead.

Until Buckaroo, Mechi had held on working in the office under the highway, she'd endured being part of the Council on the Rights of Children and Teens. But then the little pick-pocket turned up alive and without his ribs stuck into his lungs—she'd seen the photos of the pavement covered in blood and entrails—and then another boy appeared who'd been eight years old when he went missing and was eight when he reappeared, but he'd been gone for six years, so he should have been fourteen. He should have been a teenager, not a child. Then Mechi realized that she couldn't take any more, no more parents who were overjoyed at first and later grew terrified, no more news about psychiatric hospitalizations, no more staring eyes of kids in the park, sitting on the grass, on the steps, on the jungle gyms, playing with stray cats and even trying to get into the fountain. Mechi organized files, Mechi couldn't explain this supernatural return, Mechi just wanted to turn back time.

. . .

Mechi had made her decision to quit when she invited Pedro to have dinner that night. She'd disconnected the cable because she didn't want to keep listening to the hysteria on TV about the returned children. Internet was enough: she could spend hours reading news and theories and visiting chat rooms, though she never participated, in an attempt to maintain some shred of sanity. She had gone to Vanadis's MySpace page several times. The messages had stopped suddenly, all except the ones from Negative Zero, the tattoo artist. His last message, left several days before, said, "I'm coming to see you tonight."

She was also worried about moving. She didn't have the money to rent another apartment, she hadn't saved—her salary hadn't permitted it—so she would have to go back to live with her parents. She'd already checked with them, and they seemed delighted at her return. She was sorry to leave her apartment. It had a beautiful tub that she'd never used because she needed to fix a leak, and hadn't found the time or motivation to call someone to do the work. Any other time, the owner, who was very fussy, surely would have grumbled about the deterioration of the place, which Mechi had been renting for almost two years: the holes in the walls, from the balcony to the bedroom, drilled so she could install cable and watch TV lying in bed. The gray stain on the white wall above the computer, which someone had explained was normal—the heat from the machine, the fan, something like that—but that looked awful, and that she'd only made worse by trying to clean it with water. Another stain was a real disaster: the remains of red wine vomit in the hallway on the way to the bedroom, the result of an early morning of drunkenness and blackout. Mechi remembered a guy had walked her to the front door of the building but she hadn't let him up, and even that she'd gone to the kiosk and bought Migral for her headache and a Coca-Cola for her hangover, but she'd never been able to remember that vomit she found when she woke up the next morning, with a radiant migraine and all her clothes on, even her boots. She found the vomit there, stinking, and her keys still in the lock. Luckily, no one had taken them; luckily, none of her neighbors had noticed, because they would have gotten paranoid and called the cops.

But now it was possible the owner wouldn't say a thing. It was even possible he wouldn't charge her the last months of rent. People were behaving very strangely since the kids had come back, with a depressive indolence that was clear in the vacant stares of the kiosk vendors who apathetically let people run off with candy, or the subway employees who, if you didn't have change, would let you through for free. There was a deafening calm everywhere, a vast silence on the buses, fewer phone calls, the TV kept on until late in apartments. Not many people went out, and no one went near the parks where the kids lived. The kids still didn't do anything, they were just there. Months after the first return, one thing had become clear: the kids didn't eat. At first, people brought them fruit and pizza and baked chicken, and the kids accepted it all with a smile, but they never ate in front of the cameras or the neighbors who brought them meals. Over time, a more daring cameraman, plus a few people with their own cameras, had started filming the kids' daily habits. They did sleep, but they never ate or drank. They didn't seem to need water for washing, either, or at least they never bathed, they just played with the water in the public fountains and ponds in the parks. No one wanted to talk about that, because it was unspeakable that the kids didn't need nourishment. There was even a sense of calm that descended when a storekeeper near Avellaneda Park declared that the kids had broken into his supermarket at night and stolen a bunch of canned goods and dairy products. But then it turned out to be a common robbery, and the kids responsible lived in the nearby housing projects. When the story about the supermarket was disproved, the city went back to holding its breath, back to its insomniac waiting.

Pedro arrived on time: they'd agreed on ten o'clock, and he was there at ten. That was strange, not just because he wasn't a punctual person, but because the newspaper usually kept him working on last-minute issues. No more: the paper was in suspended animation, like nearly everything else. Another example was the delivery boy who brought their pizza: he rang the doorbells of other apartments before reaching Mechi's, muttering an apology and saying he'd lost the paper where he'd written down the apartment number. He nearly left without giving them change, not in an attempt to keep the money, but because he wasn't paying attention.

Mechi commented on the delivery boy's attitude to Pedro while she sliced the pizza—there was that too: they never came cut into portions anymore—and Pedro shook his head and opened a bottle of wine. He seemed firmly determined to get drunk, hoping for anesthesia and oblivion.

"Mechi, *mamita*, what the fuck is all this?" he asked after the first sip of wine. "I swear, I had information on the traffickers, on the pimps, and all of a sudden these kids turn up like nothing happened, and it all falls apart. They ruined years of work. As if it wasn't real. But I swear to you that my investigation is real—dammit, not only mine! You see how far the prosecutor got!"

"Did she quit?"

"She's in the process."

"And the video of Vanadis?"

"That devil child. I'm going to sell it to a TV show. They

give me the money and I swear I'm off to live in Montevideo, or Brazil, that's it, that's it. Come with me, Mechi, this is some *mandinga* shit, as my grandmother used to say."

"The other day I read something online that I thought . . . I don't know, it's dumb."

"Don't spend too much time online, it'll drive you crazy. But tell me."

"I don't remember well, but it's something like this. The Japanese believe that after people die, their souls go to a place that has, so to speak, limited space. And when all the places are taken, when there's no room for any more souls, they're going to start coming back to this world. And that return heralds the beginning of the end of the world, really."

Pedro was silent. Mechi thought of the photo she'd seen of Buckaroo with his chest stuck to the pavement and his legs cut in three places.

"The Japanese sure have a real-estate-focused idea of the great beyond," Pedro finally said.

"A lot of people in a small country."

"But yeah, Mechi, it could be. It could be that they're coming back. It could be anything, I don't know what to believe anymore. Last night I went to the Death House, the Caseros Prison."

"You went to look for Vanadis's friend?"

"Yeah, well . . . I don't know why I went. It's pointless to find her now, right? I went to see what's up. And you know what's there? No one."

"How can there be no one? It was full of cracked-out kids, I went near there several times, there were druggies everywhere."

"Everyone in the neighborhood says the same thing, and I tell them to go look, like I did. There's no one left. I went in during the day, because I'm crazy but not that crazy, and there are clothes everywhere, cardboard, mattresses, even a couple of tents—check out the orphans with tents, one was a Doite, some fucked-up middle-class runaway. But no people. I heard something, I saw a shadow moving fast, then I freaked out and left."

"Must've been a dog."

"What do I know, it could have been anything. Seriously, there's no one there anymore. It's like they all ran away."

They were silent. They'd barely touched the pizza.

"You're really going to leave Buenos Aires?"

"I don't want to be in this city full of ghosts with everyone going crazy, I can't take it, Mechi. Why are you staying?"

"I don't have a cent to my name."

"But I do and I'll lend you money. . . . Let's leave for a while, until something happens. I can't stand this waiting—have you realized everyone's waiting for something? They're going to set the kids on fire. They're going to gas them, set the cops on them, I don't want to see any of that. Or else the kids are going to start attacking people."

"Sounds like you've been spending a lot of time online too."

"Well yeah, that's how I know it'll drive a person nuts. I'm getting out of here until whatever has to happen has happened, and it would be good if you came with me."

Mechi was quiet as she looked at Pedro. His right leg was shaking like it was on a spring. He touched his hair so much it was greasy. No, she wasn't going anywhere with Pedro.

Plus, she wanted to stick around and see what it was that had to happen.

"Will you come with me, dear?"

"No."

"Damn, you're stubborn."

"How do you know it's only here?"

"Because it is! It's only in Buenos Aires, you know it's here. Go to Mar del Plata and there's nothing like this, don't play dumb."

"No, I mean, how do you know it's not going to start happening in other places?"

"You're diabolical, Mechi. What are you imagining, some kind of apocalypse with walking dead? A lot of these kids weren't dead, let's start there. Quit it with the internet."

They said goodbye with a long hug when Pedro left in the early morning. He'd decided to go to Brazil, to stay with a friend who worked at a newspaper in São Paulo and who would love to have a journalist from Buenos Aires who'd witnessed the children's return—because, of course, the case was already known internationally. Before leaving, he told her his boss had authorized the long, four-week vacation without blinking, almost relieved. Pedro told Mechi he felt like his boss didn't want him around. Like the guy was afraid of him.

. . .

Mechi noticed right away that her parents were a little checked out, like most people she came in contact with, but also that, while they helped her settle her things into her room—the one that had been hers ever since she was little—they were very curious to find out more, learn details, ask questions. She could feel their disappointment and a trace of disbelief when she told them she didn't know anything, that she really was just as disconcerted as everyone else. The movers finished unloading her few pieces of furniture into a storage shed in back; her parents' house was in a good neighborhood, Villa Devoto, with a lot of space, even a small swimming pool. Now that she was there, Mechi felt like it was a good place to rest.

And it was far away from the parks, and that was good, too. Very good.

Quitting her job had started out quite normal, with the council's director assuring her that he understood perfectly. He was a reasonable man and he seemed sincerely shaken; there were circles under his eyes and a broken blood vessel in the left one. When she went to the office to get her things, the situation got a bit more strange. Graciela wasn't there, for starters. Maria Laura, the other front-office employee, told her, with an ire she couldn't contain, that Graciela had requested psychiatric leave, who knew if she was going to come back, that she was having serious panic attacks and couldn't get out of bed. "Poor Graciela," said Mechi. And then Maria Laura threw a paperweight at her. Mechi barely had time to duck, and then she stood staring: Maria Laura, with her hair dyed an ugly, wine-colored shade, her face furious, her buck teeth, tensed neck—a gargoyle in an office under the highway.

"Get out of here before I kill you!"

"What's wrong, what's wrong with you?"

And Maria Laura started screaming at her uncontrollably that it was all Mechi's fault, she was the one who'd brought that little whore, that piece of trash, she was the one who'd brought her from the park that morning, Graciela was crazy and it was Mechi's fault, and she, Maria Laura, was going to end up sick because of her too, and then you have the nerve to come here for your things, we should have burned them, you should be in jail, I don't know, you started all this with that trashy whore, they should have killed you both but this shitty government won't do anything, nothing nothing. . . .

Mechi ran out with the few things she'd managed to gather stuffed into her purse. In any case, she didn't keep too much in her desk drawers. She was sorry to leave the archive, but she couldn't have taken it with her, it wasn't hers, and anyway Pedro had left her his copies of some of the files, including Vanadis's, before he got on the plane to Brazil.

In a way, she understood Maria Laura. She needed to blame someone, and Mechi *was* the one who'd brought Vanadis in, and that was the beginning of the kids coming back. What did disturb her was that she'd felt like she was in danger. Maria Laura would have been capable of killing her. The only thing that stopped her was that Graciela was just a little crazy, and the kids in the parks didn't do anything, and for better or worse she was still at work. The paperweight, though, had been aimed right at Mechi's head, and it could have hit her. Quitting had been an excellent idea.

She waited for the 134 bus that would take her to Villa Devoto on a corner across from the park. She could barely see the kids, because that area had an embankment and they never came too close to the edge, they tended to wander around inside. The startling thing was that, in the past, the sidewalk that circled Chacabuco Park had been dotted with dozens of joggers at all hours of the day, and along with the athletes were people headed for the subway entrance near the rose garden across the avenue, and neighbors walking their dogs. Now the sidewalks were deserted, and the subway entrance was closed until further notice. She was the only person waiting for the bus. The driver passed the park going double the speed limit, and only when he left it behind did he start driving at a more reasonable speed. Mechi realized it was a miracle he'd stopped for her.

. . .

The first night at her parent's house was mostly quite pleasant, except that after dinner they headed to the living room sofa and turned on the TV. Mechi didn't want to stay, and her parents got annoyed. "You can't avoid reality," they told her, and she ignored them and locked herself in her room. She knew what they were waiting for: they wanted to see, repeated over and over as the news channels always did, the report about the parents who had committed suicide in El Palomar. The girl had run away three years ago after what was apparently a savage argument: her father had hit her. When she came back—she was one of the girls at Rivadavia Park—she had a swollen eyelid and her lower lip was split and bleeding, as if the beating had occurred twenty-four hours before. She was small, with short blond hair and a nose ring. Mechi knew about the father's beating from the archive and she figured the journalists must have that information too, but when the girl came back they didn't include it in their report, they just showed the emotional reencounter and wondered aloud, "I wonder how Marisol fell down?" Then they asked her directly, and she said, "I didn't fall," and that was it. They didn't ask if someone had hit her. To Mechi, that selective silence was proof that they knew about the father's beating, and they weren't talking about it because . . . of course, because the beating had happened three years before. Years during which Marisol had maintained the exact same length and color of her hair as the day she ran away.

Sometimes Mechi trembled with rage at such cowardice, such fatuousness. She wanted someone to start shouting on TV, to howl, to say, "This is weirder than shit, who are these kids, who *are* they?"

Now she regretted having wished for the dam to break. Because it was happening, and the hysteria was extreme. The mother and father had gotten into bed together, a photo of baby Marisol between them. He had shot himself first, in the temple. Then she took the gun from his hand, put it in her mouth, and blew her brains out. They left a note that said what so many parents had said before them: "That is not our daughter."

Marisol left after the gunshots. The neighbors saw her come out, and they ran her off wielding sticks and rocks. One of them even shot at her from a distance. Was this the beginning of the hunt that Pedro had hinted at? Until that moment, the parents had simply returned their children, and if they couldn't manage the bizarre situation, at the most they were checked in to psychiatric hospitals, and the kids went back to the parks. Nor did the parents give details about why cohabitation had been so unbearable. It was known that some TV and radio programs, and even newspapers and magazines, were willing to pay for interviews with these parents who returned their kids, but, remarkably for people as loquacious and media-savvy as *porteños*, none of them wanted to talk.

The El Palomar suicide hadn't been the only one. Some days before, Mechi had gone back to Vanadis's MySpace page in search of the tattoo artist. And she had found a new message from him, after many days of silence. It said: "i went to see you but you're not you. You have white vampire teeth remember how we played, the girl I saw didn't recognize me she's a copy, she doesn't have your mouth, I can't take it I can't take it. Bye vanadis, maybe we'll meet again, my love?"

That "maybe we'll meet again" put Mechi on the alert, and she clicked on Negative Zero's profile. It wasn't hard to deduce from the comments of the tattoo artist's friends that he had killed himself. She left the page when her eyes filled up with tears. She couldn't allow herself to cry over a thirty-year-old man who had fallen in love with a child of fourteen. She shouldn't feel pity for him. He cared about the girl, sure, but he was sick. She could, though, cry for herself. Because she had never felt anything remotely like what the tattoo artist felt for Vanadis.

Negative Zero's suicide went unnoticed. After the couple in Palomar, though, voices started to emerge. The dead parents' neighbors said that ever since the girl had come home, they could hear the mother wailing all night long, nonstop. A butcher had asked the father about Marisol and he'd said everything was fine, it was just that the girl was very quiet. Everyone mentioned how Marisol never went out. Others accused her, saying the parents never would have killed themselves, they were believers and were very proper, and Marisol must have killed them. Then the floodgates opened. Other parents started to tell their own stories, their justifications for abandoning their children after they'd been reunited. Mechi didn't want to listen: somehow it seemed unfair to the kids. Maybe they were monsters, who knew what they were, but they deserved shelter, it was unfair for them to have to sleep outside like animals.

That's what she thought during the day. But at night, with the muffled sound of her parents' television and the copies from the archive under her bed, she saw Vanadis's smile of twisted teeth, and thought about that video she'd never seen—which would probably be on TV any day now if Pedro had managed to sell it—and she thought she wouldn't let that girl in her house, either, that inert girl with her black hair and ghastly smile, that girl she'd almost fallen in love with and who now appeared in her nightmares.

. . .

Marisol's parents' suicide and the neighbors' reaction—as the days passed they were calling for lynchings, or at least the execution of the girl they claimed was a murderer—was the catalyst for change. Or rather, for the migration. The kids began to leave the parks. They went in processions, in the middle of the night, through the fog: the exodus occurred in winter. As they marched through the streets, people came out onto balconies to watch them. Someone shouted an insult, but others hushed him. The withdrawal was silent. As silently as they had come, they left. They walked down the middle of the streets as if they weren't afraid of cars. The police, out of precaution or because they didn't know what to do, closed the main streets to traffic. It lasted several days. Pedro sent Mechi an email from São Paulo, where he was now the resident expert on the returned Argentine children (Pedro always managed to make things work out in his favor). The email said:

I saw it all on TV. Creepy, *mamita*. Here everyone is going crazy, these *brazucas* aren't scared at all, they're not wimps like we are, and they want to go and see it all from up close. People are different here, super cool, you've got to come, they'll change the way you think. Anyway, as I was saying, you know what this procession of kids made me think of? How in Paris they moved the cemeteries at the end of the 18th century. Really weird. Apparently the cemeteries were crammed to bursting and they were sites of infection, just filthy, and then people decided to put all the bones underground and move the cemeteries to the outskirts of the city. They moved those bones for years, at night, in carts, with black blankets on the horses so they would fit the tone, and monks singing, and candles, of course. You'll be wondering how I know all this, and it's just because when I had the cash to go to Europe of course I went to the Catacombs!!! And they explain it all there. I always imagined it kind of like this.

I got pretty fixated on what you said about the Japanese who think that when there's no more room for souls, they come back. The bones in the Catacombs are kinda like that, they ended up under there because there was no more room in the cemeteries. I don't know, weird shit. Don't have nightmares. Come visit me. No, better yet, stay there and tell me all about it.

Mechi thought about the monks and the bones, and she understood what Pedro meant. The kids' withdrawal was funereal and had something religious about it.

The strange thing was where they went. The first group, from Rivadavia Park, set the course: First they separated, and then each column went into a different abandoned house. Three hundred kids went into the house with the palm tree on Calle Riobamba, right downtown. Another three hundred went to the corner of Igualdad, in the Cafferata neighborhood of Chacabuco Park, into a house whose pink color was fading from neglect. It had a solitary window up close to the A-frame roof that the kids left open when they went in. The neighborhood, small and newly rich, was terrified, but the police in their sentry booths on the corners didn't know what to do, and once the kids were inside, they didn't dare try to get them out.

They didn't even go with a warrant.

They were scared. They didn't understand how the kids had gotten into that house. The door and windows of the pink house—except that middle window—were bricked up, and the kids had still gotten in. No one could say how. People had watched them enter, but they claimed the kids hadn't gone through the bricks, not exactly. They had just passed, as if the bricks didn't exist.

The leader of the Cafferata group was Vanadis, whose family had disowned her two weeks after they'd joyfully picked her up. They'd given the same argument that all the families gave when they kicked their kids out or deposited them on a courthouse doorstep, or returned them straight to the parks: This isn't the girl we knew, this isn't our baby. We don't know who she is. This person looks like her, has her voice, answers to the same name, she's the same down to the last detail, but she isn't our daughter. Do what you want with her. We don't want to see her ever again.

Mechi learned about Vanadis and the pink house through the newspaper. There was a photo of the girl in the first-floor window, peering out, her mouth shut and her eyes staring straight into the camera. Mechi felt dizzy looking into those eyes, and her hands started to sweat. She wanted to see Vanadis, ask her questions, how stupid not to have done it when she'd found her on the steps of the park fountain. She wanted to talk to Vanadis even though now she was very afraid of her, because she was sure that the real Vanadis was the one in the video, a teenager murdered by potbellied men in a sordid hotel on the city's outskirts, used and exterminated, a teenager who thought she was streetwise and took too many risks, putting her faith in the immunity her beauty provided.

She'd seen the video on TV. Pedro had sold it successfully, and he'd let her know when it would be on. The girl's face was clear, and it was Vanadis. And though Pedro thought that girl in the video could be alive, Mechi was sure that she wasn't. The tattoo artist's last words had convinced her: in the video the girl's mouth was half-open and you could see her large, sharp, pointed teeth, those vampire teeth the tattoo artist had mentioned. Could time have ruined them? Not that much. Not like that. The reappeared Vanadis's teeth were not just yellow: they were broken, twisted. To Mechi, that was the proof that Vanadis was dead and the girl at the pink house wasn't her, but she still wanted to see her, wanted to talk to her—she needed to.

The bus ride was strange. People kept their distance, avoided touching each other, as if the others were carrying some contagious disease. Mechi hadn't told her parents where she was going. She didn't want to worry them. She had gone out with just her keys in her pocket and told them she was going for a walk in the English quarter, the prettiest part of Villa Devoto. But what she really did was run to the avenue and take the 134. Why had she run? Lately she felt like her parents were watching her. Once, even, while she was asleep, she heard the door of her room close, as if they'd been spying on her. She thought they were a little afraid of her. It was almost time to move, to leave her childhood home again.

The perimeter of Cafferata was being guarded: Mechi could just picture those middle-class families she'd met over the years she'd worked there, they must have gone crazy straightaway, because they were incapable of comprehending any interruption to their comfortable lives. Still, the police let her through. They were pale and trembling. They would scatter at the slightest odd signal from the kids in the house, Mechi was sure. If that happened, would they send in the army? Would they kill them all, as Mechi had seen one mother call for on TV, claiming the kids were like shells, they had nothing inside?

Maybe. But not yet.

Mechi stopped on the sidewalk in front of the pink house, on the side of the small window that was still open. The sun was out, it was a cold but clear winter day, with the sky a blinding light blue. She cupped her hands around her mouth and shouted Vanadis's name. She vaguely heard the sound of blinds and doors moving restlessly at other houses, she even heard a policeman come closer, but she paid no attention. She stared straight at the white window, waiting.

Vanadis's head appeared, that face of a Central American goddess, a teenage Bianca Jagger, and she greeted Mechi with an almost imperceptible gesture. There was recognition in her dark eyes. Mechi wanted to say something, but her trembling body and pounding heart wouldn't let her speak. She breathed deeply until she calmed down and could get words out, although her voice emerged shaky and much higher than usual.

"Hi, Vanadis. What are you all doing? Why did you go in there?"

Vanadis didn't answer. Mechi asked her how many they were, and Vanadis said a lot, that she couldn't tell, it was dark. Mechi asked where they came from, and Vanadis said they came from many different places. She asked if Vanadis wanted to go back to her parents, and Vanadis said no, and added that none of them did. And then she said, louder and more clearly, as if she were finally answering the first question:

"We all live up here."

And other kids started to appear, their faces forming a circle around Vanadis. Mechi recognized most of them, teenagers and children, runaways and abductees, living and dead.

"Are you going to stay up there long?"

All together, the kids replied: "In summer we'll come down." Mechi felt then that they weren't children, that they formed a single organism, a complete being that moved in a herd. The hands of the policeman from the corner took hold of her shoulders and Mechi screamed, startled. She'd been about to hit him but held back when she saw it was a cop, a man around sixty years old—why didn't they send someone younger?—who was just as scared as she was, or even much more.

"Miss, please leave."

"No, I have to ask them more questions."

"Don't force my hand, please." The cop had taken her by the waist and the shoulders, and though he was an older man, he was strong, strong enough to drag her far away from the pink house.

"Okay, I'm going, let go of me," cried Mechi, but he didn't, he went on dragging her. Voices started to shout from neighboring houses, requests of "Officer, get her out, leave us alone," and some people even banged on windows. Mechi lost sight of the pink house, and with a cry of effort she wrenched free of the policeman's embrace and ran toward Asamblea, thinking that she was going to go far away before summer arrived, before the kids came down. Maybe she'd join Pedro, get someplace where children didn't come back from wherever it was they had gone.

The Dangers of Smoking in Bed

Was it a nocturnal butterfly or a moth? She had never been able to tell the difference. But one thing was sure: nighttime butterflies turned to dust in your fingers, as if they had no organs or blood, almost like the still cigarette ash in the ashtray if you barely touched it. It wasn't gross to kill them and you could leave them on the floor, because they disintegrated in just a few days. Another thing: it wasn't true that they immediately burned up when they got too close to heat. Someone had told her that's what happened, they caught fire as soon as they brushed against a hot bulb, but she had seen them hit against the lamp bulb over and over, as if they enjoyed the impact, and be left unhurt. Sometimes they got bored and flew out the window. Others, it was true, died inside the floor lamp: they got tired, or maybe they gave up or their time came. Just as they did outside, they burned up slowly, fluttering against the shade until they lay still. Sometimes she got up in the middle of the night to empty the lamp of dead butterfly-moths, when the burnt smell made her nose sting and wouldn't let her sleep. Rarely did she remember to turn out the light before going to bed.

But one night in early spring it was another kind of burning smell that woke her up. Wrapped in the gray travel blanket she used when it was chilly, she checked the kitchen to see if she had left anything on a lit burner. It wasn't coming from there. Nor was it the moths—she'd turned off the light that night. The smell wasn't coming from the hallway of the building, either. She raised the blinds. Outside, there was smoke and rain. Something was burning in the rain and she could hear the fire truck siren and the murmur of some neighbors in the street, awakened in the early morning, surely with raincoats thrown over their pajamas. She heard one of them, a man with a cracked voice, say, "Poor woman." The fire was far away, and Paula went back to bed. Later, she learned from the ever-informed doorman that it had been a fifth-floor apartment in a building around the corner that burned. There was one casualty, a paralyzed, bedridden woman who had fallen asleep in bed with a lit cigarette between her fingers. Her daughter, who took care of her—and who was fairly old herself, around sixty—had realized too late, when the smoke woke her up coughing, choking, and she couldn't save her mother. "Poor lady, it's an infernal habit," said the doorman, and he added that the woman smoked a lot and never went out. Paula wanted to ask him,

"How do you know the woman smoked so much, when you've just told me she never went out? When did you ever see her smoking then, huh?" But she kept her mouth shut because it was impossible to argue with the doorman, and because she was starting to picture how the woman on the fifth floor must have watched the flames climb up from her feet, and since she couldn't feel anything in her legs, she must have let the blanket burn. And surely she must have thought, Why not just let the fire keep going and do its job? It must be painful, but how long could it be before a woman like her, old and with exhausted lungs, would faint? What a relief for the daughter, too.

The doorman pulled her from that vaguely soothing world of burnt old women, bringing her back to the landing to inform her that during the week a guy was going to come through and fumigate the apartments. Paula told him great, and then she decided that if she heard the doorbell she was going to let the fumigator in. Although there weren't that many bugs in her apartment, except for the butterfly-moths, and she was sure the poison wouldn't kill them because they didn't live there, they came in from the street. Nothing lived in her house, not even the plants, which had assiduously died in recent weeks, one after another. She was the only living thing in her house.

She said goodbye to the doorman and went straight to bed. The sheets were imbued with the smell of chicken cutlets. She had made two in the oven the night before. It had been hard to wrest them out of the freezer because the plastic bag was stuck to the ice. She had to use very hot water, almost boiling, and some of the drops had burned her bare legs. It turned out to be a fruitless method, and then she tried to pry them out with a knife, and she laughed at herself through tears of self-pity, thinking that she must look like a serial killer as she stabbed at the freezer, her arm up and the knife coming down like an ice pick. Finally she extracted the cutlets, her hands numbed from cold, and put them into the oven. They burned a little, but aside from that they were barely edible because they were infused with other foul flavors: the oven leaked gas, and she hadn't cleaned it once in the three years she'd been renting the place. So she hadn't been able to eat them, and now she was hungry again and the apartment stank and the smell wouldn't let her sleep and she hated it, so much that she had to cry, and she cried because of the smell, because the incense she lit to get rid of it reeked even worse, because she never remembered to buy air freshener—which also smelled terrible—and because the cigarettes must also make everything stink but she couldn't tell because she smoked so much, and because she had never been able to have one of those clean and luminous houses that smelled of sunlight, lemons, and wood.

She made a tent in the bed, propping up the sheet with her knees and covering her head. Underneath, the only light came from the tip of her cigarette, which trembled and seemed to rekindle when the smoke whirled around it. The sheets were all stained by ashes. Paula opened her legs, and with the index finger of her free hand she started to caress her clitoris, first in circles, then with a vertical motion, then with delicate tugs, and finally side to side. It didn't work at all anymore; used to be she would feel the start of that shiver right away, and the heat of the blood rushing and then her finger could feel the skin of the vulva grow a little rougher, granulated, and with the great final tremor came the wetness, she really felt like she peed herself—that's how it used to be. But for so long now nothing happened, and she rubbed to the point of irritation and pain but stopped before the blood came; she knew that blood was the only wetness she could still squeeze out of herself.

She put the bedside lamp under the sheets. Her inner thighs were dotted with small, superficial red spots; it looked like an irritation from heat or allergy, but it was something called keratosis, and she also had it on her arms, her hips, and a little on her ribs. The dermatologist had told her that with a lot of treatment it could get better, that it was nothing like more terrible conditions like psoriasis or eczema, but she thought it was plenty terrible, just like her yellow teeth and the blood that flowed every morning from her gums when she brushed her teeth—not a momentary bleeding, real streams of blood that dripped into the white sink. It was called periodontitis, though these days dentists used another, fancier name that she couldn't remember now. Anyway, she preferred the truth, she preferred periodontitis. Her body was failing in many more ways that she didn't want to think about. Who would ever love her like that, with dandruff, depression, zits on her back, cellulite, hemorrhoids, and everything dry, so dry.

She lit another cigarette under the sheet and used the smoke to chase a butterfly that had snuck into her refuge, until it died. So you could suffocate them with smoke? What a weak and stupid animal. She let it convulse between her legs, and she saw the butterfly-moth's legs that looked like tiny maggot-worms; for the first time she felt disgust, and she kicked it out of her bed and onto the floor. She made smoke rings inside the tent until she got bored, then decided to touch the ember to the sheet and watch as the orange-edged circle grew until it seemed dangerous, until the flame crackled and rose. Then she put out the fire on the sheet by hitting it, and the remnants of burnt cloth floated in the tent. She laughed at the small circular fires. If she poked her head out of the tent and peered into the semidarkness of her room, the burnt circles in the sheet let the lamplight through, and the beams shone onto the ceiling so it seemed to be covered in stars.

She had to burn more holes, because as soon as she saw that, she knew the only thing she wanted was a starry sky over her head. It was the only thing she wanted.

Back When We Talked to the Dead

At that age there's music playing in your head all the time, as if a radio were transmitting from the nape of your neck, inside your skull. Then one day that music starts to grow softer, or it just stops. When that happens, you're no longer a teenager. But we weren't there yet, not even close, back when we talked to the dead. Back then, the music was at full blast and it sounded like Slayer, *Reign in Blood.*

We started with the Ouija board at the Polack's house, locked in her room. We had to do it in secret because Mara, the Polack's sister, was afraid of ghosts and spirits. She was afraid of everything—man, she was a stupid little kid. And we had to do it during the day, because of the sister in question and because the Polack had a big family and they all went to bed early, and the whole Ouija board thing didn't go over well with any of them because they were crazy Catholic, the kind who went to mass and prayed the rosary. The only cool one in that family was the Polack, and she had gotten her hands on a tremendous Ouija board that came as a special offer with this magazine on magic, witchcraft, and inexplicable events that was part of a series called *The World of the Occult*; they sold them at newspaper kiosks and you could collect and bind them. Several issues had already had promotions for Ouija boards, but they always ran out before any of us could save the money to buy one. Until the Polack started to take the thing seriously and really tightened her belt, and then there we were with our lovely board, with its numbers and letters in gray, a red background, and some very satanic and mystical drawings all around the central circle.

It was always the five of us who met: me, Julita, Pinocchia (we called her that because she was thick as wood, the slowest in the whole school, not because she had a big nose), the Polack, and Nadia. All five of us smoked, so the planchette seemed to be floating on fog as we played, and we left a terrible stench in the room the Polack shared with her sister. Plus, it was winter when we started with the Ouija board, and we couldn't even open the windows because we'd freeze our asses off.

And that was how the Polack's mother found us: shut in with all the smoke and the planchette going all kinds of crazy. She kicked us all out. I managed to salvage the board—it stayed with me after that—and Julita kept the planchette from breaking, which would have been a disaster for the poor Polack and her family, because the dead guy we were talking to right then seemed really evil. He'd even said he wasn't a dead spirit, but a fallen angel. Still, by that point we knew that spirits are some crafty liars and we didn't get scared anymore by their cheap tricks, like guessing birthdays or grandparents' middle names. All five of us pricked our fingers with a needle and swore with blood that we didn't move the planchette, and I believed it was true. I know I didn't. I never moved it, and I really believe my friends didn't either. It was always hard for the planchette to start moving at first, but once it got going it seemed like there was a magnet connecting it to our fingers. We barely even had to touch it, we never pushed it, not even a nudge; it slid over the mystical drawings and the letters so fast that sometimes we didn't even have time to jot down the answers to the questions (one of us always took notes) in the special notebook we kept for just that purpose.

When the Polack's crazy mom caught us (and accused us of being satanists and whores, and called all our parents: it was a clusterfuck), we had to stop the game for a while, because it was hard to find another place where we could keep going. At my house, impossible: my mom was sick in those days and she didn't want anyone in the house. She could barely stand my grandmother and me, and she would straight up kill me if I brought friends home. Julita's was no good because the apartment where she lived with her grandparents and her little brother had only one room, which they divided with a wardrobe to make two rooms, kind of. But it was just that space, no privacy at all, otherwise just the kitchen and bathroom, plus a little balcony full of aloe vera and crown-of-thorns plants—impossible any way you looked at it. Nadia's place was also impossible because it was in the slum: the other four of us didn't exactly live in fancy neighborhoods, but no chance in hell would our parents let us spend the night in a slum, they would never go for that. We could have snuck around and done it without telling them, but the truth is we were also a little scared to go. Plus, Nadia didn't bullshit us: she told us it was really rough where she lived, and she wanted to get the hell out of there as soon as she could, because she'd had it with hearing the gunshots at night and the shouts of the drunk gauchos, and with people being too scared to come visit her.

So we were left with Pinocchia's place. The only problem with her house was that it was really far away, we'd have to take two buses, plus convince our parents to let us go all the way out to East Bumfuck. But we managed it. Pinocchia's parents pretty much left her alone, so at her house there was no risk of getting kicked out with a lecture on God. And Pinocchia had her own room, because her siblings had already left home.

So finally, one summer night, all four of us got permission and went to Pinocchia's house. It was really far, her house was on a street that wasn't even paved, with a ditch running alongside it. It took us like two hours to get there. But when we did, we realized right away that it was the best idea in the world to make the trek all the way out there. Pinocchia's room was really big, with a double bed plus bunk beds: all five of us could sleep there, easy. It was an ugly house because it was still under construction: unpainted plaster, lightbulbs hanging from ugly black cords, no lamps, and a bare cement floor, no tile or wood or anything. But it was really big, with a terrace and a barbecue pit, and it was much better than any of our houses. It sucked to live so far away, sure, but if it meant having a house like that—even an unfinished one—it was worth it. Out there, far from the center of Buenos Aires, the night sky looked navy blue, there were fireflies, and the smell was different, like a mixture of burnt grass and river. Pinocchia's house had bars on all the windows, it's true, and it also had a giant black dog guarding it. I think it was a rottweiler, and you couldn't play with it because it was so mean. It seemed that living far away had its dangers too, but Pinocchia never complained.

Maybe it was because the place was so different—because that night in Pinocchia's house we did feel different, with her parents listening to Los Redondos and drinking beer while the dog barked at shadows—that Julita got up the nerve to tell us exactly which dead people she wanted to talk to.

Julita wanted to talk to her mom and dad.

It was really good that Julita finally spoke up about her folks, because we could never bring ourselves to ask. At school people talked about it a lot, but no one ever said a thing to her face, and we jumped to her defense if anyone came out with any bullshit. The thing was that everyone knew Julita's parents hadn't died in any accident: Julita's folks had disappeared. They were disappeared. They'd been disappeared. We didn't really know the right way to say it. Julita said they'd been taken away, because that's how her grandparents talked. They'd been taken away, and luckily the kids had been left in the bedroom (no one had checked the bedroom, maybe: anyway, Julita and her brother didn't remember anything, not of that night or of their parents either).

Julita wanted to find them with the board, or ask some other spirit if they'd seen them. She wanted to talk to them, and she also wanted to know where their bodies were. Because that question drove her grandparents crazy, she said; her grandma cried every day because she had nowhere to bring flowers to. Plus, Julita was really something else: she said that if we found the bodies, if the dead told us where they were and it turned out to be really real, we'd have to go on TV or to the newspapers, and we'd be famous and everyone in the world would love us.

To me, at least, Julita's cold-bloodedness seemed really harsh, but I thought, Whatever, let Julita do her thing. What we for sure had to start doing, she told us, was coming up with other disappeared people we knew, so they could help us. In a book on how to use the board, we'd read that it helped to concentrate on a dead person you knew, to recall their smell, their clothes, their mannerisms, their hair color, construct a mental image, and then it would be easier for the dead person to really come. Because sometimes a lot of false spirits would turn up and lie to you and go around and around in circles. It was hard to tell the difference.

The Polack said that her aunt's boyfriend was disappeared, that he'd been taken during the World Cup. We were all surprised because the Polack's family was really uppity. She explained that they almost never talked about the subject, but her aunt had told her once in confidence, when she was a little drunk after a barbecue at her house. The men were getting all nostalgic about Kempes and the World Cup, and the aunt got pissed off, downed her red wine, and told the Polack all about her boyfriend and how scared she'd been. Nadia contributed a friend of her dad's who used to come for dinner on Sundays when she was little, and one day had just stopped coming. She hadn't really noticed that friend's absence, mostly because he used to go to the field a lot with her dad and brothers, and they didn't take her to games. But her brothers noticed it more when he didn't come around, and they asked their old man, and the old man couldn't bring himself to lie to them and say they'd had a fight or something. He told the boys that the friend had been taken away, same thing Julita's grandparents said. Later, Nadia's brothers told her. At the time, neither the boys nor Nadia had any idea where he'd been taken, or if being taken away was common, or if it was good or bad. But now we all knew about those things, after we saw the movie *Night of the Pencils* (which made us bawl our eyes out; we rented it about once a month) and after the *Nunca Más* report on the disappeared—which Pinocchia had brought to school, because in her house they let her read it. Plus there was all the stuff we read in magazines and saw on TV. I contributed with our neighbor in back, a guy who'd lived there only a short time, less than a year. He didn't go out much but we could see him moving around out the back windows, in his little backyard. I didn't remember him much, it was kind of like a dream, and it wasn't like he spent a lot of time in the yard. But one night they came for him, and my mom told everyone about it, and she said that thanks to that son of a bitch they could have easily taken us too. Maybe because she repeated it so much, the thing with the neighbor stuck with me, and I couldn't relax until another family moved into that house and I knew he wasn't ever going to come back.

Pinocchia didn't have anyone to contribute, but we decided we had enough disappeared dead for our purposes. That night we played until four in the morning, and by then we were starting to yawn and our throats were getting scratchy from so much smoking, and the most fantastic thing of all was that Pinocchia's parents didn't even come knock on the door to send us to bed. I think—I'm not sure, because the Ouija consumed my full attention—that they were watching TV or listening to music until dawn, too.

After that first night, we got permission to go to Pinocchia's house two more times that same month. It was incredible, but all our parents or guardians had talked on the phone with Pinocchia's parents, and for some reason the conversation left them totally reassured. But we had a different problem: we were having trouble talking to the particular dead people we wanted—that is, Julita's parents. We talked to some spirits, but they gave us the runaround, they couldn't make up their minds yes or no, and they always stopped at the same place: they'd tell us where they'd been captured, but then they wouldn't go any further, they couldn't tell us if they'd been killed there or if they'd been taken somewhere else. They'd talk in circles, and then they'd leave. It was frustrating. I think we talked to my neighbor, and he got as far as naming the detention center Pozo de Arana, but then he left. It was him, for sure: he told us his name, we looked him up in *Nunca Más,* and there he was, on the list. We were scared shitless: it was the first certified for-real dead guy we'd talked to. But as for Julita's parents, nothing.

It was our fourth time at Pinocchia's when what happened happened. We'd managed to communicate with someone who knew the Polack's aunt's boyfriend; they'd gone to school together, he said. The dead guy we were talking to was named Andrés, and his story was that he hadn't been taken away and he hadn't disappeared: he'd escaped on his own to Mexico, and he died there later in a car accident, totally un-related. Well, this Andrés guy was cool, and we asked him why all the dead people took off as soon as we asked them where their bodies were. He told us that some of them left because they didn't know where they were, and they got ner-vous, uncomfortable. But others didn't answer because some-one bothered them. One of us. We wanted to know why, and he told us he didn't know the reason, but that was the deal, one of us didn't belong.

Then the spirit left.

We sat for a beat thinking about what he'd said, but we decided not to give it too much importance. At first, when we'd started playing with the board, we always asked the spirit that came if any of us bothered it. But then we stopped doing that because the spirits loved to run with the question, and they'd play with us. First they'd say Nadia, then they'd say no, everything was cool with Nadia, the one who both-ered them was Julita, and they could keep us going all night, telling one of us to put our fingers on the planchette or take them off, or even to leave the room, because those fuckers would ask us for all kinds of things.

The episode with Andrés left enough of an impression, anyway, that we decided to go over the conversation in the notebook while we cracked open a beer. Then there was a knock at the door. It startled us a little, because Pinocchia's parents never bugged us.

"Who is it?" asked Pinocchia, and her voice came out a bit shaky. We were all shitting ourselves a little, to tell the truth.

"It's Leo. Can I come in?"

"Hell yeah!" Pinocchia jumped up and opened the door. Leo was her older brother who lived downtown and only visited their parents on weekends, because he worked every weekday. And he didn't even come every weekend, because sometimes he was too tired. We knew him because before, when we were little, first and second grade, sometimes he came to pick up Pinocchia at school when their parents couldn't make it. Then, when we were big enough, we started to take the bus. A shame, because then we stopped seeing Leo, who was really fine, a big dark guy with green eyes and a murderous face, to die for. And that night, at Pinocchia's house, he was hot as ever. We all sighed a little and tried to hide the board, just so he wouldn't think we were weird. But he didn't care.

"Playing Ouija? That thing's fucked up, I'm scared of it," he said. "You girls have some balls." And then he looked at his sister: "Hey, kiddo, can you help me unload some stuff from the truck? It's for the folks, but Mom already went to bed and Dad's back is hurting ..."

"Aw, don't be a pain in the ass, it's really late!"

"Well, I could only make it out here just now, what can I say, the time got away from me. Come on, if I leave the stuff in the truck it could get lifted."

Pinocchia gave a grudging okay and asked us to wait for her. We stayed sitting on the floor around the board, talking in low voices about how cute Leo was, how he must be around twenty-three by now—he was a lot older than us.

Pinocchia was gone a long time, and we thought it was strange, so after half an hour Julita offered to go see what was going on. Then everything happened really fast, almost at the same time. The planchette moved on its own. We'd never seen anything like it. All by itself, really, none of us had a finger on it, not even close. It moved and wrote really quickly, "Ready." Ready? Ready for what? Just then we heard a scream from the street, or from the front door—it was Pinocchia's voice. We went running out to see what was going on, and we found her in her mother's arms, crying, the two of them sitting on the sofa next to the phone table. Just then we didn't understand a thing, but later, when things calmed down a little—just a little—we more or less put it together.

Pinocchia had followed her brother down to the corner. She didn't understand why he'd left the truck there when there was plenty of room by the house, but he didn't answer any of her questions. He'd changed as soon as they left the house, he'd turned mean and wouldn't talk to her. When they got to the corner he told her to wait, and, according to Pinocchia, he disappeared. It was dark, so it could be that he walked a few steps away and she lost sight of him, but according to her he'd disappeared. She waited a while to see if he would come back, but since the truck wasn't there either, she got scared. She went back to the house and found her parents awake, in bed. She told them Leo had been there, that he'd been acting really weird, and that he'd asked her to help unload things from his truck. Her parents looked at her like she was crazy. "Leo wasn't here, sweetie, what are you talking about? He has to work early tomorrow." Pinocchia started trembling with fear and saying, "It was Leo, it was Leo," and then her dad got all worked up, and shouted at her and asked if she was high or what. Her mom was calmer, and she said, "Listen, let's call Leo at home. He's probably asleep, but we'll wake him up." She was doubting a little now too, because she could tell that Pinocchia was really positive and really upset. She called, and after a long time Leo answered, cursing, because he'd been fast asleep. Their mom told him, "I'll explain later," or something like that, and she started to soothe Pinocchia, who was having a terrible meltdown.

They even called an ambulance, because Pinocchia couldn't stop screaming that "the thing" had touched her (an arm around the shoulders, in a sort of hug that had made her feel more cold than warm), and that it had come for her because she was "the one who bothered them."

Julita whispered into my ear, "It's because she didn't have anyone disappear." I told her to shut her mouth—poor Pinocchia. I was really scared, too. If it wasn't Leo, who was it? Because that person who'd come to get Pinocchia looked exactly like her brother, he was like an identical twin, and she hadn't doubted for a second either. Who was it? I didn't want to remember his eyes. And I didn't want to play with the

Ouija board ever again, let me tell you, or even go back to Pinocchia's house at all.

Our little group never got together again. Pinocchia was hit really hard, and her parents blamed us—poor things, they had to blame someone. They said we'd played a mean prank on her, and it was our fault she went a little crazy after that. But we all knew they were wrong; we knew the spirits had come to get her because, as the dead guy Andrés told us, one of us bothered them, and it was her. And just like that, the time when we talked to the dead came to an end.

PHOTO: © NORA LEZANO

MARIANA ENRIQUEZ is a writer and editor based in Buenos Aires, where she contributes to a number of newspapers and literary journals, both fiction and nonfiction.

ABOUT THE TYPE

This book was set in Walbaum, a typeface designed in 1810 by German punch cutter J. E. (Justus Erich) Walbaum (1768–1839). Walbaum's type is more French than German in appearance. Like Bodoni, it is a classical typeface, yet its openness and slight irregularities give it a human, romantic quality.